"*Daniel, I never stopped loving you.*"

His eyes hardened. "If you had loved me, you would never have walked out. You don't know what it is to love, Julie. It isn't in the core of stone hanging where your heart should be."

Her mouth trembled. Daniel had to know how difficult it was for her to bare her soul to him. "If you honestly believe that, there's no point in having this discussion."

Abruptly, she stood and hurried out of the room. Shimmering tears blurred her vision as she made her way to the parking lot.

Before she reached the vehicle, a male hand suddenly gripped her upper arm and turned her around.

"Running away again?" Daniel rasped. "I won't let you this time. You're marrying me, Julie, as soon as I can make the arrangements!"

Dear Reader,

Welcome to Silhouette. Experience the magic of the wonderful world where two people fall in love. Meet heroines who will make you cheer for their happiness, and heroes (be they the boy next door or a handsome, mysterious stranger) who will win your heart. Silhouette Romances reflect the magic of love—sweeping you away with books that will make you laugh and cry, heartwarming, poignant stories that will move you time and time again.

In the next few months, we're publishing romances by many of your all-time favorites, such as Diana Palmer, Brittany Young, Emilie Richards and Arlene James. Your response to these authors and other authors of Silhouette Romances has served as a touchstone for us, and we're pleased to bring you more books with Silhouette's distinctive medley of charm, wit and—above all—*romance*.

I hope you enjoy this book and the many stories to come. Experience the magic!

Sincerely,

Tara Hughes
Senior Editor
Silhouette Books

DEBBIE MACOMBER
Yesterday Once More

Silhouette Romance

Published by Silhouette Books New York

America's Publisher of Contemporary Romance

For my brother, Terry Adler,
who was responsible for my first "best seller."
He made copies of my diary and sold them to
the boys in my eighth-grade class.
And to his saintly wife, Miki,
With Love

SILHOUETTE BOOKS
300 E. 42nd St., New York, N.Y. 10017

ISBN: 0-373-08461-7

First Silhouette Books printing October 1986

America's Publisher of Contemporary Romance

Printed in the U.S.A.

DEBBIE MACOMBER

has quickly become one of Silhouette's most prolific authors. A wife and mother of four, she not only manages to keep her family happy, but she also keeps her publisher and readers happy with each book she writes.

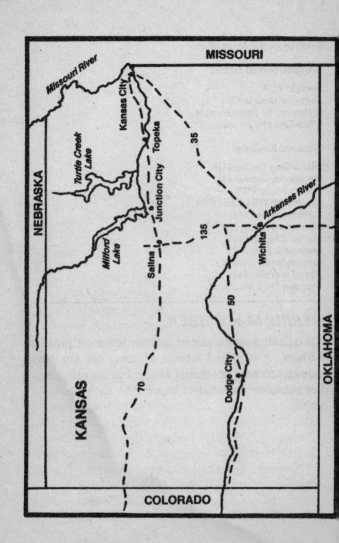

Chapter One

Julie Houser pushed the elevator button and stepped back to wait. An older woman whose office was on the same floor joined her and they exchanged lazy smiles.

Absently Julie glanced at her watch; she'd have plenty of time to finish unpacking tonight. Not wanting to take the trouble to cook a meal, she toyed with the idea of stopping off and picking up something simple from the local drive-in.

The giant metal doors swooshed open and then the two women moved to the rear of the elevator, anticipating the five-thirty rush. By the time the car emptied on the bottom floor it would be filled to capacity.

The next floor down it stopped again. This time three men boarded. Julie's concentration was centered on the lighted numbers above the door when the elevator came to a third halt. Another man entered and absently Julie squeezed herself into the far corner to make room.

The strap of her purse slid off her shoulder and as she eased it back up she felt someone's eyes roam over her. Accustomed to the appreciative gaze of men, Julie ignored the look and the man. The close scrutiny continued and she could all but feel the heated stare that started at the top of her shoulder length chestnut-colored hair and ran over her smooth oval features. Color seeped into her high cheekbones and the gentle curve of her mouth tightened. Abruptly Julie turned her head, her blue eyes snapping.

But after one look at her admirer, she nearly choked. She felt chilled and burning at the same moment. Her heart rate hammered wildly like that of a captured fledgling. The whole world came to a sudden, jangling halt. Her hand tightened around the purse strap as if the flimsy piece of leather would hold her upright.

"Daniel." The name slipped from her lips as her eyes met and held those of the man standing closest to her. His dark eyes narrowed and an impassive expression masked his strikingly handsome features.

Unable to bear his impassive gaze any longer, Julie lowered her eyes, her long lashes fluttering closed.

The elevator stopped and everyone filed out until she stood alone in the empty shell, her breath coming in deep, uneven gasps as her throat filled with a painful hoarseness. So soon? She'd only been back to Wichita six days. Never had she dreamed she'd see Daniel so quickly. And in her own building. Was his office here? *Oh, please*, she begged, *not yet; I'm not ready.*

"You coming or going?" An irritated voice from the large foyer broke into her thoughts and Julie moved on unsteady legs out of the elevator.

Her heels clicked noisily across the marble floor and the echo was deafening. The downtown sidewalks were filled with people rushing about and Julie weaved her way through the crowds uncertain where she'd parked her car that morning. Pausing at a red light, she realized she was walking in the wrong direction and turned around. Ten minutes later her hand trembled uncontrollably as she placed the key in the car door and turned the lock.

Her heart felt as if she'd been running a marathon as she slipped into the driver's seat and pressed her forehead against the steering wheel. Nothing could have prepared her for this meeting. Three long years had passed since the last time she'd seen Daniel. Years of change. She'd only been nineteen when she'd fled in panic. He had cause to be bitter and she was sorry, so terribly sorry. The regret she felt for hurting the man she loved so intensely was almost more than she could bear.

And she had loved Daniel. The evening he'd slipped the diamond engagement ring on her finger had been the happiest of her young life. No one should ever expect that kind of contentment at nineteen.

Julie let her thoughts drift back to that night as she started her car and headed toward her apartment. Daniel had taken her to an elegant French restaurant. The lights were dim, and flickering candlelight sent shadows dancing over the white linen tablecloth. Julie tried not to reveal how ill-at-ease she was in the fancy place. She had been so worried that she'd pick up the wrong fork, or worse, dump her soup in her lap. She was so much in love with Daniel and she desperately wanted to please him.

"Happy?" he asked.

Julie glanced over the top of the gold-tasseled menu and nodded shyly. Everything on the menu was written in French with an English translation below. Even with that she didn't know half of what was offered, having never sampled frog legs or sweetbreads. "What would you suggest?"

Daniel set his menu aside, his thoughts occupied. Julie noticed that from the moment he picked her up that evening he'd been unnaturally quiet. Nerves tightened the sensitive muscles of her stomach.

"Daniel, is something the matter?" she ventured, fighting off a troubled frown.

He stared at her blankly and shook his head.

"I'm not wearing the right kind of dress, am I?" She'd changed outfits three times before he'd arrived, parading each one in front of her mother until Margaret Houser had demanded that Julie stop being so particular. Any one of the outfits was perfectly fine.

"You're beautiful," Daniel whispered and the look in his eyes confirmed the softly murmured words.

Pleased, Julie lowered her gaze until her thick lashes fluttered against the high arch of her cheek. Her hand smoothed an imaginary crease from her crisp skirt. "I wanted everything to be perfect tonight."

"Why?"

Julie's tongue felt thick and she answered him with a delicate shrug of one shoulder. She wanted everything to be perfect for Daniel every time. "You've been very quiet," she noted. "Have I done something to upset you?"

His deep, resonant chuckle sent her heart rate into double time. "Oh, my sweet, adorable Julie, is it any wonder I love you so?" His hand reached for hers, gripping her fingers with his on top of the table. "I've been trying to find a way to ask you a question."

"But, Daniel, all you need to do is ask."

He sighed expressively. "It's not that simple, my love."

Julie couldn't imagine what was troubling him. Daniel was usually so thoughtful that he did everything possible to make her comfortable. When they met his friends, he kept her at his side because he knew she was a bit reserved. A thousand times over the last six months, he'd been so loving and caring that it hadn't taken Julie long to lose her heart to him. Slowly he'd brought her into his world. He often took her to the Country Club and had taught her how to play golf and tennis. Gradually his friends had become hers until the reticent Julie had flowered under his love.

But a blossom had its season and soon wilted and drooped. Maybe Daniel was trying to think of a way to gently let her down. Maybe he was tired of her. Maybe he didn't want to see her again. Panic filled her mind and she tightly clenched the linen napkin in her lap, praying that she wouldn't make a fool out of herself and burst into tears when he told her.

"I've been accepted into the law practice of Mc-Fife, Lawson and Garrison."

Julie jerked her head up happily. "That's wonderful news. Congratulations."

A smile worked its way to his eyes. "It's only a junior partnership."

"But, Daniel, that's the firm you were hoping would accept you."

"Yes, it is, for more reasons than you know."

Her hand tightened around the stem of her waterglass. Now she understood why he'd chosen such an expensive restaurant. "We're here to celebrate then."

"Not quite yet." He leaned forward and clasped her hand with both of his. "Honey, these last months have been the happiest of my life."

"Mine, too," she whispered.

"I know you're only nineteen and I probably should wait a couple of years."

Julie's heart was pounding so loudly she was afraid he could hear it. Briefly, her eyes met his. "Yes, Daniel?"

"What I'm trying to say is . . . I love you, Julie. I've never made any secret of how I feel about you. Now that I've been accepted into the law firm and can offer you a future, I'm asking you to marry me."

The words came to her like a gentle, calming breeze after a turbulent storm. Julie closed her eyes savoring the warmth of his words.

"For heaven's sake," Daniel growled. "Say something."

Julie bit into her bottom lip, convinced if she said anything, she'd start to cry.

"Julie," he pleaded.

She nodded wildly.

"Does that mean yes?"

The words trembled from her lips. "Yes, Daniel, yes! I love you so much. I can't think of anything that would make me happier than to spend the rest of my life with you."

The loving look in Daniel's eyes was enough to melt her bones. "I didn't think anything could be so heavy," he said pulling the jeweler's box from his coat pocket. He opened the lid and the size of the diamond caused Julie to gasp.

"Oh, Daniel." Unbidden tears blurred her gaze.

"Do you like it? The jeweler assured me that we can exchange it if you want."

"It's the most beautiful ring I've ever seen."

"Here." He took her hand again and slowly slipped the diamond onto her finger, his eyes alight with a heart full of love....

Battling to put an end to the memories that were flooding her thoughts, Julie pulled into the apartment parking lot and sat for several long moments. Absently, her fingers toyed with the gold chain that hung around her slender neck, seeking the diamond. She kept the engagement ring there and would continue to wear it all her life until it was back on her finger where it belonged. But after seeing Daniel today, Julie realized how difficult the task was going to be. Daniel wouldn't forgive her easily. With a determined effort she climbed out of her car and walked to her apartment.

Uninspired and drab best described her quarters. The bright, sunny apartment she'd left in California had been shared with good friends, people who loved and appreciated her.

Resolutely, she'd returned to the unhappiness facing her in Wichita. She had no choice.

The most difficult decision she'd ever made was to flee Wichita three years ago. The second hardest was to come back. But she had no option. Love demanded that she return and set things right—if possible.

Julie hung her purse on the bedroom doorknob and placed her coat in the closet. Several large boxes littered the living room floor, but she felt exhausted, the kind of fatigue that had nothing to do with physical exertion.

Everything had happened just as she'd hoped. The job had been lined up even before the move, then in a relatively good area, she'd located an apartment within her budget. The transition had been a smooth one. But to have inadvertently run into Daniel after only six days seemed unreal. That she hadn't counted on. She sat on the couch and rested her head against the back cushion.

Straightening, Julie moved onto the floor and crawled along the carpet until she located the box that contained their engagement portrait. With a sense of unreality, she stared at the two smiling faces. They'd been so much in love. Tears filled her eyes and the happy faces swam in and out of her vision.

Lovingly her fingers traced Daniel's face. The smiling good looks had disappeared. The years had added a harshness to him, an arrogant aloofness. Even the sandy-colored hair that had always seemed to be tousled by the wind was urbanely styled. The powerful male features were apparent even then, but more pronounced now. Her finger idly moved over the lean, proud jaw and paused at the tiny cleft in his chin.

A sad smile touched her eyes as the memories rolled back. She had loved to kiss him there. To tease him unmercifully with her lips. And he had been so wonderful. Conscious of her innocence, Daniel had held his desire in tight rein. Julie wondered if he regretted that now. The opportunities to make her completely his had been many but Daniel had been the one to put a stop to their foreplay, never letting things develop beyond his control. She'd respected him and loved him for that until her heart ached. He wouldn't accept the ring when she tried to return it. Julie wore it around her neck. It rested at the hollow between her breasts, near her heart. Daniel would always be close to her no matter how many miles separated them. Or how much pain.

Early the next morning Julie arrived at work intent on checking the occupant listings of the office complex. The Inland Empire Building housed fifteen floors of offices. The directory was against the wall in the foyer.

Daniel Van Deen, Attorney seemed to leap off the register at her. Again Julie experienced that hot, cold, chilled, burning feeling. Only one floor separated her from Daniel. For five of the six days since she'd been in Wichita they'd crossed paths without even knowing it. A multitude of questions and doubts buzzed through her mind like bees around an active, busy hive.

Unexpectedly a tingling sensation swept through her and she didn't need to be told that Daniel had entered the building. Slowly she turned her head to see him walk to the elevator, a newspaper clenched under his arm. He pushed the button and almost immediately the wide doors opened. Stepping inside, he turned around. Their eyes clashed and locked from across the width of the foyer.

Shivering, she watched an angry frustration sweep over his features. His magnetic dark eyes narrowed as he stared back at her. A muscle leaped uncontrollably in his cheek before the huge doors glided shut.

Julie released a quivering breath, unaware that she'd been holding one in. Daniel hadn't forgotten or forgiven her. The look he'd given her just now had sliced into her heart like the jagged edge of a carving knife.

Her legs felt unsteady as she took the next elevator and stepped into the office of Cheney Trust and Mortgage Company. Grateful that she was the first one to arrive that morning, Julie sat at her desk, striving to regain her usual poise. Her hand trembled visibly as she opened the bottom desk drawer and deposited her purse.

Sherry Adams, a pert blonde, strolled in about fifteen minutes late. Their employer, Jack Barrett, had arrived earlier and pointedly stared at the empty desk, noting Sherry's absence. Julie had only been working at the office a few days, and although Sherry had her faults, it was easy to see that the young divorcee was a valuable asset.

"Morning," Julie responded to the warmth in her co-worker's voice. "You look like the cat who got into the cream."

"I am." She gave a brilliant imitation of a fashion model, her skirts flaring as she whirled around for effect.

"I take it you want me to guess?" Julie asked, falling prey to Sherry's playfulness.

"Not really. I just thought you'd be interested in knowing that I was recently asked to dinner by the most eligible man in town."

"Congratulations."

"Thank you. Actually this is the culmination of five weeks of plotting and fine-tuning some basic womanly skills. I must admit that this guy has been one tough fish to catch."

"Well double congratulations then," Julie said with a soft laugh.

Sherry sat and rolled her chair over to Julie's desk. "I don't suppose...you-know-who...has arrived." Sherry quirked her head toward the closed door of their employer's office.

"'Fraid so, about fifteen minutes ago."

"Did he say anything about me being late?" she asked, but didn't look the least bit concerned.

"Not to me he didn't."

"One of these days, old Barrett is going to fire me, and with good reason."

"I doubt that," Julie commented with confidence. "Now tell me about your hot date."

"It's with Danny Van Deen."

Julie bit back a gasp of shocked disbelief and lowered her gaze, hoping to hide her surprise.

"He's a lawyer in the building," Sherry continued. "Cagey fellow, but I've set my sights on him for a long time now. He's only taken the first nibble, but I swear it won't be long before I reel him in."

"Good luck." Julie forced her voice to maintain the same level of cheerfulness.

"Of course I can't let him know I'm interested. That would be the kiss of death as far as Danny's concerned. Maintaining a cool facade shouldn't be so difficult. By the time we're standing at the altar he'll think it was all his idea."

"I, uh, I thought you were soured on wedded bliss."

"Not me. It didn't work out with Andy. I feel badly about that, but we both just fell out of love with each other. Not much either one of us could do about it, really."

"And...this Van Deen...has he been disillusioned with marriage?"

"Nope. That's the amazing thing. Danny's never married. I can't understand it either. He's perfect husband material: handsome, intelligent and sensitive under that cool exterior of his. He dates often enough, but nothing ever comes of it. Until now." She laughed softly. "I'll have him to the altar before he knows what hit him."

"Best wishes then." Somehow Julie managed to murmur the words.

"I'm going to need all the luck I can get," Sherry added and made a pretense of straightening her desk. "Are you taking first lunch today?"

"If you like," Julie replied absently as she flipped through the pages of a report she was studying.

"Would you mind cutting it short so I could get out of here by twelve-thirty? I'll make up the time for you later, I promise." Sherry's brilliant blue eyes contained a pleading look. "There's a dress I saw in a boutique window and I want to try it on. That's the reason I was late this morning. Wait until Danny Van Deen sees me in that." She rolled her eyes dramatically.

"Sure," Julie agreed. "I can be back early."

The remainder of the morning was peaceful. The two women took turns answering the phone. Because she wasn't fully accustomed to the office, Julie relied on Sherry for help, which the blonde supplied willingly. Sherry was a generous soul who harbored no ill against anyone. That's what made her divorce so difficult to understand. Julie couldn't imagine her new-found friend giving up on anything as important as a marriage.

A couple of minutes after noon Sherry reminded Julie of the time. Julie stood, ready to leave for her lunch break. As she took her purse out of the desk drawer, her boss, Jack Barrett, strolled into the outer room.

"Are you going out for lunch?" the balding, middle-aged man asked Julie.

"Would you like me to get you something?" she volunteered.

"Not today." He handed her a large manila envelope. "But would you mind dropping this off at Daniel Van Deen's office?"

Chapter Two

Panic filled Julie's eyes as she cast a pleading glance at Sherry.

"Go on. You might catch a glimpse of him and then you'll know what I mean when I say hunk!" Apparently Sherry believed Julie's reluctance was due to the claim she'd staked on Daniel.

"Is there a problem?" Jack Barrett glanced from one girl to the other.

"No problem," Sherry answered on Julie's behalf.

With little way to gracefully bow out of the situation, Julie nodded her agreement.

"His office is one floor down. Number 919, I think." Sherry bit her bottom lip. "Yes, 919, I'm sure of it. Not to worry, his name's on the door."

Julie forced a smile and walked out of the office. By the time she rode the elevator and got off on Daniel's floor the envelope felt as if it weighed fifty pounds.

The palm of her hand felt clammy as she turned the knob and walked into the plush office.

A round-faced secretary glanced up and smiled. "Can I help you?"

The first thing Julie noticed about the woman was her diamond ring. She was married. Why it should matter to her that Daniel's secretary was married was beyond Julie.

"I . . . have a package for Mr. Van Deen from Jack Barrett," she managed at last.

"Agnes, did you find—" Abruptly, Daniel stopped midsentence as soon as he caught sight of Julie. The hard look in his eyes was directed solely at her.

For a crazy second, Julie imagined this was the way Daniel would look before going into battle. Intent and intense, prepared to lay down his life for the sake of righteousness. Then unexpectedly his gaze softened and an emotion Julie couldn't define came over his features.

"Mr. Barrett's sent the papers you asked about this morning," Agnes supplied.

Although Julie heard Daniel's secretary speak, she felt as if she and Daniel were trapped in a hazy fog that swirled around the room.

"You did ask about the Macmillan papers?" The woman's words seemed slurred and distant.

"Yes." Daniel broke the spell, but his dark, unreadable eyes continued to hold Julie captive.

The secretary took the envelope out of her frozen hand. The woman's sharp gaze went first to Julie then to Daniel. "Was that all?"

"Pardon?" Julie tore her attention from Daniel.

"Was there something else?"

"No," she mumbled. "Thank you."

A puzzled look marred the woman's brow. "Thank you for bringing them," she murmured.

Julie turned and managed to walk out of the office with her head held high.

The remainder of the day passed in a blur and by the time she returned home that night, Julie felt physically and mentally drained.

The first thing to greet Julie as she walked into her apartment was her new phone. The installer had apparently come by. The first person she decided to call was her mother.

"Hi, Mom," she greeted with a falsely cheerful note.

"Julie. How are you?"

"Fine. Everything's fine."

"I'm so glad, dear. I've been worried."

Margaret Houser lived in a retirement community in Southern California. None of Julie's family was in Wichita anymore. Her older brother lived in Montana, but both Julie and Joe, her brother, had been born and raised in Kansas.

"Have you looked up any of your old high school friends?"

"Not yet." Actually Julie doubted that she would. The only real friends she'd had in Wichita had married and moved elsewhere. "Mom." She took in a deep breath. "I've seen Daniel."

Instantly, her mother was concerned. "How is he?"

"We...we haven't talked. But he's changed. In some ways I hardly know him. He never understood why I left. He's not likely to understand why I came back."

"Don't be so sure, sweetheart." Margaret's soft voice was reassuring. "He's been hurt, and the years are bound to have changed him."

"Mom, I don't think he will talk to me."

"I've never known you to be a defeatist," her mother said in a confident, supportive tone. "But I worry about Daniel's mother. Be careful of her."

"I will." Idly Julie's fingers flipped through the white pages of the telephone directory as they spoke. Clara Van Deen's phone was unlisted. But Daniel's was there. Her mother continued to speak, and Julie made a few monosyllabic replies as her finger ran back and forth over Daniel's name. The movement had a strange calming effect on her, as if she was reaching out to him.

"Did you hear me, Julie?"

The remark pulled Julie back into the conversation. "I'll be careful of Mrs. Van Deen, I promise."

"The woman can be completely unreasonable. Remember I was the one who had to deal with her after you left."

"I know and I'm sorry about that."

"You did the right thing, honey."

Julie wasn't sure. After three years, she still didn't know. She'd been so stupid, so naive. A hundred times she should have said something. She'd wanted to put a stop to the outrageous wedding plans. But like Daniel, she had been caught in the overwhelming force of his mother's personality. Even when she did tell Mrs. Van Deen how she felt, her wishes were pushed aside.

"Julie, are you there?" Margaret asked.

"Yes, I'm here. Sorry, Mom, it's been a long day. I'll talk to you next week."

"I'll be thinking about you."

"Thanks, Mom, I can use all the happy thoughts I can get." Her mother's love had gotten her through the most difficult times and it was sure to help her now.

"Are you sure you're doing the right thing?"

"I'm sure," Julie returned confidently.

Gently Julie replaced the receiver in its cradle. She slumped forward on the couch and buried her face in her hands. A tightness was building in her throat. It was as if three years had never passed. The anxiety was as keen now as it had been that spring.

From the beginning, Julie was aware that Daniel's mother wanted her son to marry a more socially prominent girl. But to her credit, Clara Van Deen accepted Julie as Daniel's choice. Then she immediately set about to make Julie into something she would never be. First she completely remade Julie's appearance. Clara had her hair cut and styled, then purchased an entire wardrobe of what she claimed were outfits more suitable for Daniel's wife.

Julie swallowed her pride a hundred times and tried to do exactly as Mrs. Van Deen wished. She did so want to make Daniel proud. He was a man coming up in the world and Julie didn't want to do anything to hamper his success, as his mother claimed the wrong woman would surely do.

The wedding plans were what had finally caused Julie to buckle and run. All Julie had wanted was a simple ceremony with only their immediate families. Before she knew what had happened, Daniel's mother had issued invitations to four hundred close and intimate friends she couldn't possibly insult by not inviting to the wedding.

"But, Daniel," Julie had protested, "I don't know any of these people." At the time, Julie knew that she should have told him the truth. She never knew why she didn't. Maybe it was because she was afraid he wouldn't want her if he knew how shy she actually was.

"Don't worry about it," Daniel had said and kissed the tip of her nose, never fully understanding the depth of Julie's anxieties. "They'll love you as much as I do."

Daniel had negated any further protests with a searing kiss that left Julie too weak to argue.

As the date drew closer, Julie was the focus of attention at a variety of teas and social events. She felt as if the phony smile she'd painted on her mouth would become permanently engraved on her pale features.

After each event, Mrs. Van Deen would run through a list of taboos that Julie had violated. No matter how hard Julie tried, there was always something she'd done wrong or shouldn't have said. Someone she might have offended.

"I can't take it anymore," Julie cried to her mother in a fit of tears after one such event.

"Say something," her mother advised.

"Don't you think I've tried?" Julie shouted and buried her face in her hands. "This isn't a wedding anymore, it's a Hollywood production."

Every day the pressure mounted. The whole wedding grew until what had started out as an uncomplicated ceremony was a monster that loomed ready to devour Julie. The caterers, musicians, soloist, organist. The flower girl, the dresses, the bridesmaids. Mrs. Van Deen even made the arrangements for their honeymoon.

"Daniel, please listen to me," Julie had begged a week before the wedding. "I don't want any of this."

"Honey, I know you're nervous," he'd whispered soothingly. "But everything will be over in one day and we can go on with the rest of our lives as we wish."

But Julie doubted that they could. Every incident with his mother reinforced her belief that this was only the beginning. Soon, Julie believed, Mrs. Van Deen would take over every aspect of their marriage as she had the wedding. Her suspicions were confirmed when Julie learned that Daniel's mother had made a large down payment on a house for them.

"It's her wedding gift to us," Daniel explained to Julie. But the house was only a few minutes from his mother's and the handwriting was bold and clear on the freshly painted walls. His mother insisted she would help Julie with decorating and choosing the furniture. Such things couldn't be left in the hands of an immature nineteen-year-old.

"Doesn't it bother you the way she's taken over our lives?" Julie cried.

In that second, Julie could see that Daniel did care, but would do nothing.

"For the first time since Dad died, my mother's got purpose. She's loving every minute of this. Can't you see the difference our wedding has made in her?"

No, Julie couldn't see. All she could feel was a growing case of claustrophobia. That night she couldn't sleep. By the time the sun rose early the next morning, Julie had packed her bags.

"You can't do this," Margaret Houser argued, aghast when she realized her daughter's plans.

"I've got to," Julie cried, her eyes red and haunted. "I'm not marrying Daniel. I'm marrying his mother."

"But the wedding's in five days."

"There will be no wedding," Julie replied adamantly. "What could have been a simple and beautiful ceremony has been turned into a three-ring circus and I won't be part of it."

"But Julie—"

"I know what you're going to say," she interrupted her mother. "This is far more than pre-wedding jitters. Daniel and I are never alone anymore. His mother has taken over every aspect of our relationship."

"Talk to him, dear. Explain how you feel," Margaret Houser advised. "At least do that much. This is a serious step you're considering."

Julie took her mother's advice and went to Daniel's office. They met as he was on his way out the door.

"Julie." He seemed surprised to see her.

"I need to talk to you." Her hands were clenched tightly in front of her.

Daniel glanced at his watch. "Honey, I don't have the time. Can it wait?"

"No." She shook her head forcefully. "It can't wait."

Daniel apparently had noted her agitated manner. He pressed a hand to the small of her back and led her into his office. "All right, honey, I know things have been hectic lately, but it's bound to get better once we're married. We'll have lots of time together then, I promise."

"That's just it, Daniel," Julie informed him vigorously. "We aren't going to be married."

Daniel inhaled sharply. "What do you mean?" He looked around a moment, shocked at her statement. "What's this all about?"

"I can't marry you, Daniel." Her finger trembling, she slipped the diamond off and held it out to him in the palm of her hand.

"Julie!" He was stunned. Shocked. "Put that ring back where it belongs," he muttered harshly.

"I can't," she repeated.

"I don't understand." He slumped onto the arm of his office chair.

"I don't imagine that you do." Julie bowed her head, preferring not to reveal the pain in her eyes. "Do you remember last week when I suggested we drive across the border and get married? You laughed." Her voice wobbled and threatened to crack. "But I was serious. Dead serious."

"Mother would never forgive us if we did something like that." He defended his actions.

Julie released a short, harsh breath. "I think that's the crux of the situation. You wouldn't dream of crossing your mother, but it doesn't seem to matter what all this is doing to me."

"But she loves you."

"She loves the woman she's created. Haven't you noticed anything? Look at me, Daniel," she cried. "Am I the same woman I was three months ago?"

"I don't know what you're talking about."

"Look at me," she repeated, her voice high-pitched. "My hair is different, my nails are groomed, and my...my clothes..." Tears welled in her blue eyes as her voice broke. "Did you realize I have to phone your mother every morning to ask her what she wants me to wear? I haven't had on a pair of jeans in weeks. It's unbecoming, you know," she cried flippantly, and gestured weakly with her hand. "I'm slowly being molded, shaped, carved into what she thinks would be the picture of the right woman for you. I've had it. I can't take it anymore."

Daniel stood and threaded his fingers through his hair. "Why don't you stand up to her?"

"Do you think I haven't tried? But no one listens to me. Even you, Daniel. What I think or feel doesn't seem to matter anymore. I'm...not even sure how I feel about you anymore."

"Is that so?" He exhaled a sharp breath.

"That's right," Julie insisted huskily, her chin jutting out defensively. "I want out. Here." Again she tried to return the ring.

For an agonizing moment Daniel stared at her and then the ring. With barely suppressed violence he stalked to the far side of the room and looked out the window, his back to her. He rammed his hands into his pockets. "Keep it."

"But Daniel," she pleaded.

"I said keep it," he grated. When he turned around, his mouth had twisted into a rigid line. The piercing dark eyes clouded with hurt and pain. "Now get out of my life and stay out."

Tears ran down her face. Julie turned and left. She drove straight to her mother's. The clothes, the wedding dress, everything Mrs. Van Deen had purchased was left strewn across the bed. Julie had then loaded her suitcases into the back of her car and driven to California and her aunt's.

That had been three years ago and every night since she'd wondered if she'd done the right thing. Slowly Julie straightened from her position on the sofa. The guilt had pressed down on her oppressively, but the love they'd shared had never died. At least not for Julie. She'd hurt Daniel and his mother. Right or wrong there were better ways to have handled the situation.

Now after three years, she'd come back to ask Daniel's and Mrs. Van Deen's forgiveness. She wouldn't return to California without it.

Chapter Three

The next morning Julie stood inside the Inland Empire foyer and waited until Daniel entered the building. She longed to talk to him. She'd dreamed of it for months, praying that her heartfelt apology could wipe out the pain she'd caused him. Then, only then, could they start to rebuild their crippled relationship. She'd found him so much sooner than she'd expected. Surely that was a positive sign.

As had happened previously, her body reacted to his presence even before she saw him. The tingling awareness struck the moment he pushed past the large double glass doors.

Julie straightened and watched him advance toward the elevator. If he realized she was there, he gave no outward indication. Without a sound she moved behind him so that when the metal doors glided open she could enter when he did.

Frustration knotted her stomach as two others stepped inside the tiny cubicle and the four ascended together.

If Daniel was aware of her presence he refused to react. But Julie had never been more aware of anyone or anything in her life. Daniel's tall, handsome figure, looming beside her, seemed to fill the elevator. The years had been good to him. He'd been boyishly good-looking three years ago; now he was devastating. No wonder Sherry had set her sights on him. Daniel could have any woman he wanted. However, from the information Sherry had given her, Daniel didn't seem to notice or care about his effect on the opposite sex.

A tortured minute passed and Julie yearned to reach out and touch him, anything to force him to acknowledge that she was there. He couldn't go on ignoring her forever. Sooner or later they'd need to talk. Surely he recognized that.

His gaze focused straight ahead and Julie's heart throbbed painfully as the creases around his mouth hardened. He resembled a jungle panther trapped in a cage too compact for him to pace.

Her stomach tightened in nervous reaction, but she couldn't tear her gaze from him. His features were so achingly familiar, but upon close inspection the changes in Daniel were even more prominent. Streaks of gray were mingled with the sandy-colored hair at the side of his meticulously groomed head.

Again she had to restrain herself from brushing the hair from his temple. Her legs were shaking so badly she could hardly remain upright, so she leaned against the back wall for support.

The two strangers exited on the fifth floor and a surprised Julie found herself alone with Daniel. This was exactly what she'd planned, yet her tongue suddenly felt uncooperative. There was so much she wanted to say, and she'd practiced exactly how to begin so many times. But now that the opportunity was there, she found herself incapable of uttering a single sound.

"Hello, Daniel," she managed after several awkward moments. Charged currents vibrated in the short space separating them. The high voltage added to Julie's discomfort.

He ignored her, staring straight ahead.

"We need to talk." Her voice was barely above a whisper.

Silence.

"Daniel, please."

She noted the way his mouth twisted into a hard line as he turned and directed his attention away from her.

Gently she laid her hand on his forearm. A deep sigh rumbled from her throat at the look in his eyes. The hopelessness of the situation overwhelmed her. As stinging tears filled her eyes, the tall figure that towered beside her became a watery blur, and Julie dropped her hand. The elevator stopped and she watched him leave. Daniel had refused to look at her.

Again Julie was grateful to be the first one in the office. She collapsed into her chair, fighting off waves of nausea. Pain pounded at her temple. It was too soon. She was expecting too much. Time. Daniel needed time. There was nothing she could do until he was ready to talk. She had to be patient. When he was ready, she'd be waiting.

"Morning." Sherry strolled into the office five minutes early, her eyes twinkling.

Hiding her expression, Julie feigned absorption in a paper she was studying on her desk.

"Aren't you interested in how my hot date went?"

Julie didn't want to hear any of it, but was uncertain how she could effectively disguise her feelings. "Sure." She swallowed tightly and banished the mental image of Daniel holding Sherry passionately in his arms.

"Awful," Sherry admitted with a wry grin. "Talk about disappointment! I could have had two heads for all the notice he gave me and my new dress."

"Maybe he was worried about a case or something." Julie couldn't repress a surge of gladness. If Sherry was to become involved with Daniel, the situation would be unpleasant.

"Or something, is right," Sherry shot back.

"If last night was such a disaster, how come you're so cheerful this morning?"

"Because Danny apologized and asked me out again this weekend." Sherry's voice contained a lilt of excitement. "And when he takes a woman out, believe me when I say he spares no expense. We went to the best restaurant in town. What a waste. Danny barely tasted his dinner."

Danny! Julie's mind rejected the casual use of his name. Daniel used to hate it. No one called him Danny.

"I hope everything works out better the next time," Julie replied, and smiled stiffly.

"It will," Sherry said, her voice high with confidence. "Next time, he won't be able to take his eyes off me." She paused and laughed lightly. "I won't let him." She smiled to herself, apparently over some private joke, hung her bright jacket on a hanger and placed it inside the office closet.

"Are you doing anything special this weekend?" Sherry asked as an afterthought. Her blond head tilted curiously, lighting her expressive face.

"Painting my living room walls." Filling her time was vital at the moment. Anything to keep her mind from Sherry doing her utmost to lure Daniel into falling in love with her. For part of the morning Julie debated if she should say something to her newfound friend. But what? Julie had relinquished him when she'd left Wichita. She had no right to claim Daniel now.

When Julie woke Saturday morning the sun was shining and the early spring day was glorious. Much too beautiful to spend indoors. She recalled how Daniel's mother loved to work in her flower garden. Clara Van Deen had grown the most gorgeous irises.

When Julie climbed into her car, her intention had been to drive to the paint store, but instead she found herself on the street that led to Clara Van Deen's house.

She pulled to a stop across the street and stared at the lovely two-story home with the meticulously land-scaped front yard. A fancy sports car was parked in the driveway. Julie doubted that Mrs. Van Deen would ever drive that type of vehicle. Since she was butting her head against a brick wall with Daniel, Julie debated whether she should gather her courage and approach his mother.

The long circular driveway was bordered on both sides by flowering red azaleas. Julie stared at the house for a long time, undecided about what to do. She wondered what had become of Daniel's mother. From past experience Julie realized that Clara Van Deen could be a greater challenge than her son.

Julie rubbed a weary hand over her eyes. No. Now wasn't the time. Not when she was dressed in jeans and a sweatshirt. When she faced Mrs. Van Deen she would need to look and feel her best. The desire to get the confrontation over with as quickly as possible would profit neither of them. Before her resolution wavered, she shifted gears and headed toward the closest shopping center.

The paint she chose for the living room was an antique white that was sure to cheer the drab room. Filled with purpose, her spirits lifted as she returned to the apartment. She actually looked forward to spending a quiet afternoon painting.

First she unhooked the drapes and carefully laid them across the back of the davenport. Intent on spreading out newspapers, she jerked upright as the sound of the doorbell caught her off guard. In her rush to get to the front door, she stumbled over the ottoman.

Stooping to rub her hand over the injured shin, she opened the door. "Yes?"

Daniel's tall figure towered above her and filled the doorway. The look on his face sent a cold shaft of apprehension racing through her blood.

"Leave my mother alone."

Julie stared back at him speechlessly, then slowly straightened.

"Did you hear what I said?" he demanded. Anger smoldered in his hard gaze.

Numbly she nodded.

"I saw you this morning parked in front of her house. Stay away, Julie, I'm warning you."

Inwardly Julie flinched and jutted her chin out in a gesture of defiance. "The time will come when I'll have to talk to her."

"Not if I can help it."

"You can't."

"Don't bet on it." His eyes were as frigid as a glacier snowpack.

"Daniel, I've come a thousand miles to talk to you and your mother."

"Then you wasted your time because neither one of us cares to see you."

Levelly, Julie met his gaze, realizing the task she had set before her would be more difficult than she'd thought possible. "I didn't come back to hurt you or your mother. I've come to make amends."

"Amends?" Viciously, he threw the word back at her as he paced the carpet, his hand buried deep in his pant pockets. "Do you think you could ever undo the humiliation I suffered when you walked out?"

"I'm sure I can't, but I'd like to try. Don't you understand? I was young and stupid. A thousand times I've regretted what I did—"

"Regretted." He paused and turned to face her. "I used to dream you'd say that to me. Now that you have, it means nothing. Nothing," he repeated. "I look at you and I don't feel a thing. You came back to apologize, then fine, you've made your peace. Just don't go to my mother, bringing up the past. She has no desire to see you. Whatever you and I shared is over and done with."

Julie hung her head and closed her eyes at the sting in his voice. She wouldn't be easily swayed from her goal. "Oh, Daniel," she whispered. "You don't mean that."

"Does that bother you?" he asked. "You taught me a lot of things. I've blocked you from my mind, but unfortunately my mother has never been the same. I can't forgive you for what you've done to her."

"But that's the reason I've come back," she said with forced calm. Her stomach churned violently and her eyes pleaded desperately with his. "I want to make it up to you both. Can't you see how sorry I am? I couldn't stop thinking about you. Not for a day. Not for a minute. For three long years you've haunted me."

"Do you want me to pat you on the head and tell you everything's just fine and we can pick up where we left off?" His dark eyes hardened. "It's not that easy."

Julie lowered her gaze and struggled to maintain a grip on her composure. "You've changed so much. Oh, Daniel, have I done this to you?"

His dark eyes raked her from head to toe, and Julie could see that he wouldn't answer her.

Unaware she would even do such a thing, Julie raised her hand to his mouth. Lightly her fingertips caressed his lips. Abruptly, Daniel jerked his head back and retreated a step as if she'd seared him.

"I don't want to hurt or upset you or your mother," she began softly.

"Then leave before you do both."

"Oh, Daniel, I wish I could. But this is too important to me. I've got to make things right."

"You'll never be able to do that. Sometimes it's better when the past remains buried."

"I can't. Believe me, I tried. For a long time I tried."

Daniel looked exhausted. "Leave, Julie. You could do more harm now."

"Didn't you hear what I just said? I won't go," she returned forcefully. "Not until I've talked to your mother. Not until I pay her back every penny."

"Why now?" He sank onto the sofa and leaned forward until his elbows rested on his knees.

"Just as you've changed, Daniel, so have I. I'm not a naive nineteen-year-old anymore. I'm a mature woman willing to admit I made a terrible mistake. I was wrong to have run away instead of confronting the problems we faced. I regret what I did, but more than that I realize that there isn't anyone I could ever feel as strongly about as you. All these years I've dreamed of you. When another man held me, I found myself wanting him to be you. It's you I came back for. You, Daniel."

He stared at her disbelievingly. "You mean to tell me that after all these years your conscience hasn't quit bothering you?"

"Yes, but it's so much more than that. If possible I want to make everything up to you."

"That's fine and dandy. You've come, we've talked and now you've done everything you can. Now you can go. I absolve you from everything. Just stay out of my life. Understand?"

A look of pain flashed across his face, and for a fleeting moment Julie saw a glimmer of the old Daniel. Something was troubling him, something deep and intense.

"Daniel." She moved to his side, fighting back the urge to touch him. Something was bothering him and she yearned to comfort the man she loved. Carefully, she weighed her words. "Something's wrong. Won't you tell me what it is?"

He looked right through her and Julie knew he was lost to another world.

Defiantly he stood, impatiently shaking off his mood. "Leave my mother alone. Do you understand?"

"I'm sorry." Julie hung her head. Her long, brown hair fell forward, wreathing her oval face. Everything she'd tried to explain had meant nothing.

"Julie?" A wealth of emotion weighted her name.

With controlled movements, she stood and faced him. "I promise not to do anything to hurt her. Can you trust me for that at least?"

"I shouldn't." A nerve moved in his jaw and again Julie was aware of the battle struggling inside him. Without another word, he turned and walked out of the apartment.

Numb, Julie stood exactly where she was for what could have been a split second or a half hour. Her hands felt moist with nervous perspiration. Forcing herself into action, she finished spreading the old newspapers across the floor and opened the first gallon of paint.

Julie worked until well past midnight. When she finished, the old room was barely recognizable. The feeling of accomplishment helped lift her heavy heart. Had she thought confronting Daniel and his mother would be easy? No. From the beginning she'd known what to expect.

Absently her hand fingered the ring dangling from around her neck. She was physically exhausted as she cleaned the paint brushes under the kitchen faucet, but her mind continued to work double time.

As she worked, Julie remembered Daniel's words. Maybe he was right. Perhaps contacting Clara Van Deen now could do more harm than good. Hours later, lying in bed, staring at the darkened ceiling, Julie couldn't let the thought go. She'd come this far. The clock dial illuminated the time in the dark bedroom. Two A.M. and although she was physically exhausted, she hadn't been able to sleep. Pounding her pillow, Julie rolled over and faced the wall.

Write her.

The idea flashed through her mind like a laser beam. Instantly, Julie sat up and threw back the covers and searched for a pen and pad.

Sitting on top of the bed, her bedside lamp burning, Julie drafted the letter:

Dear Mrs. Van Deen:

I know this letter will come as a shock to you. My hope is that you will accept it in the light in which it is written.

I wonder if you've ever done anything in your life that you've regretted. Something that has haunted you over the years. Something you would give anything to do over again. I have. For three years I've carried the guilt of what I did to you and Daniel. Mere words could never undo the acute embarrassment or the deep hurt my actions inflicted. I won't even attempt to make retribution with a simple apology. I would beg your forgiveness, and ask that you allow me to make this up to you in some way. Anything.

My address reads as above with my telephone number. If you desire to contact me please do so. I will await word from you.

Julie read the letter again the following morning. The next move would be Mrs. Van Deen's.

A week passed before she heard from the older woman. Seven long, anxious days for Julie. Every one of those days she saw Daniel. Not once did he speak to her, but his eyes held a warning light that said more than an angry tirade. Julie wondered if his mother had told him about the letter. With that thought came another. Would Daniel hate her all the more for not heeding his request?

The scented envelope with the delicate handwriting captured her attention the minute she picked up her mail early Saturday afternoon. Julie's heart rate soared.

She was barely inside her apartment door when she ripped open the envelope. Her fingers shook as she took out the single sheet of stationery.

It read simply: *Saturday at four.*

"That's today." Julie spoke out loud. Frantically she shot a look at the kitchen clock. Just after one. She had only three hours to prepare herself. Mrs. Van Deen had done that deliberately, hoping to catch her off guard. But Daniel's mother would be disappointed. Julie was prepared for this confrontation. She knew what had to be said and she was willing to deal with the difficult task.

After carefully surveying her wardrobe, Julie finally decided to wear a simple business suit of blue gabardine. It was the same one she'd worn to the job interview with Mr. Barrett six weeks earlier. She wanted to show Mrs. Van Deen that she wasn't an awkward teenager any longer, but a mature woman. At precisely four o'clock, Julie pulled into the curved driveway.

The doorbell was answered by Mrs. Batten, the elderly cook who had been with the family for years. If she recognized Julie, she said nothing.

"Yes?" The woman's low tone was barely civil.

"Good afternoon. I'm here to see Mrs. Van Deen."

Mrs. Batten hesitated.

"I'm expected," Julie added.

Again the woman paused before stepping aside and allowing Julie to enter the foyer.

The interior of the house hadn't changed. Everything was exactly as she remembered. The same mahogany table and vase sat beside the carpeted stairway that led to the second floor. To her left was the salon, as Mrs. Van Deen called it. At one time Julie had thought of it as a torture chamber. To her right was a massive dining room.

"This way," Mrs. Batten instructed, her tone only slightly less frosty.

Like an errant student being brought to the school principal, Julie followed two steps behind the elderly woman. She was led through the house to the back garden Mrs. Van Deen prized so highly.

"You may wait here." Mrs. Batten pointed to a heavy cast-iron chair separated from an identical one by a small table.

Julie did as requested.

"Would you like something to drink while you wait?" The woman's eyes refused to meet Julie's.

"No. Thank you," she mumbled, clasping her hands together in her lap.

Fifteen minutes passed and still Julie sat alone. Every second was another trial. Daniel's mother was doing this deliberately. Testing her. But Julie was determined to sit there until midnight if necessary.

The sound of soft footsteps behind her caused Julie to tense.

"Hello, Julie." The words were low and trembling.

Julie stood and turned around. Daniel's mother was frail and obviously weak. She leaned heavily upon a cane, her back hunched. Yet she was elegant as ever. Her hair was completely white now and she was thin, far thinner than Julie remembered.

"Sit down." Mrs. Van Deen motioned with her hand and Julie sank into the uncomfortable chair, grateful for the chair's support.

Daniel's mother took the seat beside her. Both hands rested on top of the wooden cane. "To say I was surprised to receive your letter would be an understatement."

"I imagine it was." Julie's grip on her purse tightened.

"Does Daniel know you're back?"

She nodded. "We work in the same building."

The frail woman didn't comment, but smiled weakly.

If Daniel was different it was nothing compared to the changes in his mother.

"You have a Wichita address."

"Yes, I moved back." Her voice quavered slightly.

"Why?"

"Because—" Julie swallowed around the thickness building in her throat "—because I wanted to make amends and I didn't think I could do that if I flew in for a weekend."

"That was wise, dear."

"I came because I deeply regret my actions. I—"

"Do you still love my son?" Clara Van Deen interrupted.

Julie focused her attention on her hands, tightly coiled around the small leather purse. The question was one she'd avoided since her return, afraid of the answer. "Yes," she admitted without hesitation. "Yes, I do, but I . . ."

"But you hate me?"

"Oh, no." Julie snapped her head up. "The only person I've hated over the years was myself."

The old woman's smile was wan. "There comes a time in a woman's life when she can look at things more clearly. In my life it comes as I face death. As you've probably guessed, I'm not well."

Unexpected tears filled Julie's eyes. She hadn't expected Daniel's mother to be kind or understanding.

"There's no need to cry. I've lived a full life, but my heart is weak and I can't do much of anything these days. Ill health gives one an opportunity to gain perspective."

"Then you do forgive me?" Julie asked in a mere whisper, her voice dangerously close to cracking.

The veined hand tightened around the cane. "No."

Julie closed her eyes to the disappointment and hurt. An apology would have been too easy; she should have realized that. Mrs. Van Deen would want so much more. "What can I do?" Julie asked softly.

"I want you to forgive me." Daniel's mother spoke gently and reached across the short space separating them and patted Julie's hand. "I was the reason you did what you did. All these years I've buried that guilt deep in my heart. I behaved like an interfering old woman."

Julie noticed a tear that slid down the weathered cheek, followed by several more. Her own face was moist.

"We've both been fools."

"But there's no fool like an old one." Clara Van Deen wiped her cheek with the back of her hand. She looked pale and tired, but a radiance came from her eyes.

As if on cue, Mrs. Batten carried in a silver tray with a coffeepot and two china cups. Mrs. Van Deen waited until the woman had left before asking Julie to do the honors.

A smile lit up her face as Julie poured the coffee, stirred sugar into Daniel's mother's and presented her with the first cup and saucer.

"Very good." Mrs. Van Deen nodded approvingly.

Julie laughed, perhaps her first real laugh in three years. "I had a marvelous teacher." She sat back and crossed her legs, the saucer held in her hand.

"Tell me what you've done with yourself all this time." Mrs. Van Deen looked genuinely interested.

"I went to school for a while in California and lived with my aunt. Later my mother joined me and I got a job with a bank as a teller and worked my way into the loan department. From there I got a job in a trust company. Nothing very exciting."

"What about men?"

"I...dated some." The abrupt question flustered her.

"Anyone seriously?"

Julie shook her head. "No one. What...what about Daniel?"

The former radiance dimmed. "He never tells me."

"He's changed."

"Yes, he has." Mrs. Van Deen didn't deny the obvious. "And not for the good I fear. He's an intense young man. Some days he reminds me of..." She paused and stared straight ahead.

"Mrs. Van Deen, are you feeling all right?"

"I'm fine, child. You're beginning to sound like Daniel. He's always worried about me. And please, I'd prefer it if you called me Clara."

Even when engaged to Daniel, Julie had never been allotted the honor of using Mrs. Van Deen's first name. The privilege to do so now was a confirmation of their new understanding.

"All right, Clara." The name felt awkward on her tongue.

"I do have regrets." The older woman looked as if she were in another world. "I would so have liked to hold a grandchild."

Julie took a sip of her coffee, hoping the liquid would ease the coiled tightness in her throat.

"I know what it's cost you to come to me," Mrs. Van Deen continued. "You have far more character than I gave you credit—" The woman's tired eyes widened and she paused to take in deep breaths. "I'm sorry, Julie, but I'm not feeling well." The older woman's hand covered her heart. "I think you should call Mrs. Batten."

Panic filled Julie. Daniel's mother was a lot more than weak and unwell. Clara Van Deen was on the verge of collapsing. "Mrs. Batten," she cried as she bounded to her feet and ran toward the kitchen. "Call Medic One and tell them to hurry."

Tears were streaming down Julie's face as she struggled to recall the lessons she'd taken in pulmonary resuscitation. She fell to her knees beside Daniel's mother and took the weathered hand in hers.

"Don't worry so, child," Clara assured her. The frail voice was incredibly weak. Julie had to strain to make out the words.

Julie began loosening the older woman's clothes, words of reassurance tumbling from her lips. She couldn't bear to lose Clara now. Slowly, Mrs. Van Deen was losing consciousness. Dear Lord, why was it taking the medics so long? Daniel's mother's life was held on a delicate balance as Julie lowered her to the floor and knelt at her side. The sound of sirens could be heard screaming in the distance and Julie breathed easier.

Heavy footsteps followed and Julie stumbled aside as the two men entered and began working frantically over the unconscious woman. A flurry of questions came from another team of men who brought in a stretcher and loaded Mrs. Van Deen into the waiting vehicle. Tubes and needles were inserted into Clara's arm by the trained medics.

Her own heart pounded so loudly that Julie was unable to hear any of the commotion around her. Mrs. Batten walked to the front lawn with Julie as they carried Daniel's mother to the mobile unit.

"I'm going to the hospital," Julie told the housekeeper. She'd go crazy waiting around here. For a second Julie questioned whether she was in any condition to drive. Her hands were shaking so badly she had trouble inserting the key into the ignition.

The hospital was a whirlwind of activity when Julie arrived. She almost collided with Daniel as she hurried down the wide corridor. He stopped and his look sliced into her with a fine cutting edge, as if he wanted to blame her for his mother's ill health. After a moment he entered the waiting room, leaving her standing alone in the hall.

Julie's fingers were clenched so tightly the blood flow to her fingers were severely hampered. To hide her own fears, she bit into the corner of her bottom lip.

Daniel didn't want her with him, and yet she couldn't leave without knowing what had happened.

The chapel offered her the solitude she desired. Needing the time to think, she buried her face in her hands as she sat in the back pew. Her mind was in such turmoil that clear thought was impossible. An eternity passed before Julie stood.

Daniel was pacing the small waiting area when she returned. He turned toward her as she entered the room.

"Don't ask me to leave," she pleaded.

He rammed his fingers through his hair, and not for the first time if the sandy rumpled mass was any indication. "The ambulance driver was in. He told me you were responsible for calling them in time to save her life."

Julie didn't answer. Her arms cradled her stomach as she paced the enclosure with him. They didn't speak. They didn't touch. But Julie couldn't remember a closer communication with anyone. It was as if they were reaching out mentally to each other, offering encouragement and hope when there seemed little.

The whole universe seemed to come to a stop when the doctor stepped into the room. "She's resting comfortably," he announced without preamble.

"Thank God," Daniel said with a shuddering breath.

"Your mother's a stubborn woman. She insists upon seeing both of you. But only take a minute. Understand?"

Julie glanced at Daniel. "You go."

"Both," the doctor repeated.

Clara Van Deen looked as pale as the sheets she was lying against when Julie and Daniel entered the intensive care unit.

She opened her eyes and attempted to smile when she saw they were there. "My dears," she began, "I'm so sorry to cause you all this worry."

"Rest, mother." Daniel whispered.

"Not yet." She fluttered her eyes open. "Julie, you said you'd do anything to gain my forgiveness?"

"Yes." That strange voice hardly sounded like her own.

"And Daniel, my son, will you do one last thing for me?"

"Anything, you know that." He didn't sound any more controlled.

The tired, old eyes closed and opened again as if she was on the brink of slipping away. "My dears, won't you please marry... for my sake."

Chapter Four

Julie woke in the gray light of early morning. She hadn't slept well and imagined Daniel hadn't either. They'd hardly spoken as they left the hospital and scarcely looked at one another. The white line that circled Daniel's mouth revealed his feelings in the matter of any marriage between them. Words weren't necessary.

When she'd arrived home Julie undressed and made herself a cup of strong coffee. She sat in the living room, bracing her feet against the coffee table as she slouched down on the sofa. Her thoughts were troubled and confused. Clara was so different from what she'd expected. Julie had braced herself for a confrontation, confident the older woman would lash out at her. Instead she'd discovered a sick, gentle woman who had suffered many regrets. Deep within her, Julie longed to ease Clara's mind. Daniel's mother lay weak in a hospital bed, facing death. She needed the assurance that her son would be happy.

But, Julie knew, they wouldn't have any kind of marriage when Daniel resented her so much.

Her mind continued to be troubled as she readied for bed. As she lay staring at the wall, a calm came over her. She loved Daniel, had loved him when she ran away all those years ago and, if possible, loved him even more now. Every time she looked at him, his features so lovingly familiar, her heart ached with that love. Closing her eyes, Julie reminded herself over and over again of the reasons she'd returned to Wichita.

Even at midmorning the hospital parking lot was full. Although Julie hadn't reached a decision, she had peace in her heart. She'd talk to Daniel, really talk. Together they would decide what to do.

The faint antiseptic odor greeted her as she pushed through the large double glass doors that led to the hospital foyer. The sound of her shoes clapping against the polished floor seemed to echo a hundred-fold as she walked down the wide corridor.

Daniel was in the waiting area outside the intensive care unit. He glanced up as Julie approached, his eyes heavy from lack of sleep.

"Good morning," she said in a soft tone. "How's Clara?"

"My mother," he returned stiffly, "rested comfortably."

Julie took the seat opposite Daniel. "Can we talk?" Sitting on the edge of the cushion, Julie leaned slightly forward and linked her fingers.

Daniel shrugged his muscular shoulders and ran a hand over his face.

"Did you sleep at all?"

A quick shake of his head confirmed her suspicions. "I couldn't. What about you?" he asked without lifting his gaze.

"Some." She noticed that Daniel wouldn't look at her, not directly. Even when she'd entered the room his intense gaze had met hers only briefly before focusing on something behind her.

"The doctor's with her now."

"Daniel." Julie found it difficult to speak. "What are we going to do?"

His laughter was mirthless, chilling. "What do you mean *do*? My mother didn't know what she was saying. They'd given her so many drugs yesterday she wasn't thinking straight. Today she won't remember a word."

Julie didn't believe that any more than Daniel did, but if he wished to avoid the issue there was little she could say.

They didn't speak and while his gaze was directed at the floor, Julie had the opportunity to study him. The lines about his mouth and eyes were more pronounced now, deeply etched with his concern. His brow was creased in thick furrows. Julie knew that his mother was all the family Daniel had.

A coffee machine across the hall caught her attention and Julie took several coins from her purse and stood. She added sugar to each of their cups and cream to Daniel's. His gaze bounced off her as he accepted the Styrofoam container. She watched as surprise flickered over his face and knew that he hadn't expected her to remember he used sugar and cream.

They both set the coffee aside and looked up expectantly when the doctor entered the room.

The white-haired man smiled reassuringly and Julie noticed for the first time the gentleness that seemed to emanate from the man.

"How is she?" Daniel spoke first.

"She's incredibly weak, but better than we expected. For her to have survived the night is nothing short of a miracle." The doctor paused to study them both. "Your mother seems to have decided she wants to live. And since she's come this far the possibilities of her making a complete recovery are good."

Julie bit into her bottom lip to keep from crying out with relief.

"She's resting now and from the look of things, both of you should do the same."

Daniel nodded. "I didn't want to leave until I was sure she was going to be all right."

The doctor shook his head. "I don't know what she said to you last night, but whatever it was has made the world of difference in her attitude. From that moment on, she started to recover."

Julie's eyes clashed with Daniel's. If possible he paled all the more.

"Now go home and get some rest. There's nothing you can do here. I'll phone you the minute there's any change."

"Thank you, Doctor," Daniel said, his voice husky with appreciation.

They remained standing even after the doctor left. Daniel closed his eyes and released a long, exhausted sigh.

"Can I drop you off at your place?" Julie asked quietly. Daniel didn't look as if he was in any condition to drive.

He looked at her and shook his head. "No."

"You'll phone me if you hear anything?"

He answered her with an affirmative shake of his head.

"Everything's going to work out for the best," she whispered and walked away, leaving the hospital and heading back to her apartment.

Julie didn't mean to sleep, but after arriving home and phoning her mother to tell her about Clara Van Deen's attack, she decided to stretch out on the sofa and rest her eyes a few minutes. The next thing she knew someone was knocking on the door.

Abruptly rising to a sitting position, Julie glanced at her wristwatch and was shocked to notice that it was after two.

"Just a minute," she called and hurriedly slipped her feet back into her shoes and ran her fingers through her tangled hair. "Who is it?" she asked before releasing the lock.

"Daniel," came the taut reply.

Immediately, Julie threw open the door. "Is she all right? I mean, she's not worse, is she?"

"No." He shook his head. "She's doing remarkably well."

"Thank God," Julie whispered as she stepped aside to let Daniel into her apartment.

"I do," Daniel murmured under his breath as he walked past her. "Did I wake you?"

With a dry smile, Julie nodded. "It's a good thing you did or I wouldn't be able to sleep tonight."

"They let me see her for a few minutes," he said and stood uneasily in the center of the room.

"And?" Julie prompted.

"And—" he paused and ran a hand through his thick hair, rumpling the urbane effect "—she asked when we were planning to have the wedding."

Julie walked to the sofa and sat down. "I was afraid of that."

Daniel remained standing. "Apparently she's been talking to the nurses about us. The head nurse told me she firmly believed the fact you and I are going to be married was what kept mother alive last night. It was what the doctor called her sudden will to live."

"And," Julie finished for him, "you're afraid telling her otherwise could kill her."

Daniel stalked to the far side of the room and spoke with his back to her. "I talked to the doctor again. He explained that if mother can grow strong enough in the next few months there's a possibility that heart surgery could correct her condition."

"That's wonderful news."

He turned to her then and the hard look in his dark eyes raked over her. "Yes, in some ways it's given me reason to hope. But in others..." He shook his head and let the rest of his words fade into nothingness.

"Why did you come back, Julie? Why couldn't you have left well enough alone?"

"I already explained," she answered quietly and squeezed her hands tightly together. "I want— No," she amended, "I need your forgiveness."

"My forgiveness," he repeated and lifted his head so that she could read the exasperation into his eyes. "I wish to God that I had never seen you again."

The pain of his words slammed into Julie and she struggled to disguise her response. "But I am here and I won't leave until I've accomplished that."

"You have a long wait."

"I didn't expect it to be easy."

Forcefully he muttered a curse under his breath. "I don't know what to do. I can't see us getting married. Not the way I feel about you."

"No," she agreed, "I can't see adding that complication to our relationship."

"We have no relationship." His voice grated as he stalked from the apartment.

Julie stopped at the hospital with a flower arrangement on her way home from work Monday afternoon. Since Mrs. Van Deen remained in the intensive care unit, Julie doubted that she would be able to see her. But when she reached the nurses' station she was informed that special permission had been granted for her to visit. The same five-minute limitation applied.

Clara looked pale against the white sheets. She opened her eyes and gave Julie a feeble smile.

"I'm so pleased you came," she whispered, squeezing Julie's hand.

"I can only stay a few minutes," Julie told her in a soft voice.

"I know."

"How are you feeling?"

"Much better now that I know Daniel will be happy."

A strangling sensation gripped Julie's throat. She couldn't think of any way to tell Clara Van Deen that she and Daniel weren't going to be married.

"It was all my fault, I realize that now." The frail voice wavered. "With you and Daniel married I can undo some of the harm I did."

"But..." Julie groaned inwardly. "Marriage isn't something to rush into. I'm still very much in love with Daniel, but he's been badly hurt and needs time to forget the pain I caused him."

The tired eyes fluttered closed. "Daniel loves you. He always has. His pride's been hurt, but he'll come around. I know he will."

So much for that argument, Julie mused unhappily.

"Trust me, child. The reason he's hurting so much is because he loves you."

The nurse stepped up to the bedside. "I'm sorry, but I'm going to have to ask you to leave now."

Julie leaned down and gently kissed the weathered cheek. "Rest now, and I'll stop in tomorrow afternoon."

The old eyes opened again. "Tell Daniel you love him," she whispered, her voice barely audible. "He needs to know that."

Julie didn't answer one way or the other. How could she admit something like that to a man who fought her in every way he could? Julie had more pride than to set herself up for that kind of pain.

Daniel was in the waiting room when she came into the hallway. He stood and glanced at her expectantly when she entered the area.

"She looks much better today."

He nodded, but Julie was sure he hadn't heard anything she'd said.

"Can we go someplace and talk?" he asked tightly.

The hospital cafeteria was almost empty. A few people were sitting at circular tables near the window.

"Go ahead and sit down and I'll bring us something. Iced tea?" he quizzed, arching a questioning brow.

The afternoon was sunny and warm for early spring and Julie smiled her thanks. Iced tea was her favorite summertime drink. She hadn't expected Daniel to remember that.

He carried the two tall glasses on an orange-colored tray and deposited it on a nearby table after removing their drinks.

"I talked to Dr. Berube again this afternoon," he said, staring into the tea.

Julie's hand curled around the icy glass, the cold seeping up her arm.

"The doctor seems to feel that if we...if I...was to disappoint mother about this marriage it could be extremely detrimental to her recovery."

The icy coldness stopped at Julie's heart. "Does this mean you want to go ahead with the wedding?" Her voice sounded incredibly soft.

"No." he breathed out a sigh. "A marriage between us would never work. The possibility of a life together ended when you left. But my mother's health—"

"Daniel," she said, her voice gaining volume, "I know you may find this hard to believe after all these years, but I never stopped loving you."

His eyes hardened. "If you had loved me, you would never have walked out. You don't know what it is to love, Julie. It isn't in the core of stone hanging where your heart should be."

Her mouth trembled with the effort to restrain stinging tears. She had done as Daniel's mother suggested and humbled herself. Daniel had to know how difficult it was for her to bare her soul to him and yet he tossed her declaration of love back in her face. "If you honestly believe that, there's no point in having this discussion." Abruptly, she stood and hurried out of the room. Shimmering tears blurred her vision as she made her way to the parking lot.

Suddenly, a male hand gripped her upper arm and turned her around before she reached her vehicle.

"Running away again?" he rasped. "I won't let you this time. You're marrying me, Julie, as soon as I can make the arrangements."

"I'd be crazy to marry a man like you."

His laughter was harsh. "Do you think you can carry the guilt of my mother's death on your shoulders? If you walk out now, that's what will happen.

It'll kill her. Are you ready to face that, Julie? Or don't you care?''

Julie pulled herself free from his grip. "Daniel," she pleaded, "marriage is sacred."

"Not in this instance," he insisted. "It'll be one of convenience."

"Will it remain that way?" Her questioning eyes sought his.

His steady gaze didn't flicker. "I couldn't touch you."

Biting into the soft, spongy flesh in her inner cheek, Julie struggled not to reveal the hurt his honesty had inflicted. It shouldn't matter to her. The way he felt about her, Julie didn't want Daniel to make love to her. "And after your mother..." She couldn't bring herself to mention the possibility of Clara Van Deen's death.

"You will be free to go, no strings attached. An annulment will be fairly simple."

"I don't know." Julie smoothed a hand across her forehead. "I need time to think."

"No," Daniel shot back sharply. "I need to know now. This minute."

In some ways he was right. What choice did she have? Slowly, deliberately, Julie nodded her head. "All right, Daniel, I'll marry you, but only for your mother's sake."

His lip curled up sardonically. "Do you think I'd marry you otherwise?"

"No, I don't suppose you would." Unfastening the chain from around her neck, Julie handed him her original engagement ring.

"You kept it?" Shock rang through his voice.

Julie stared wistfully into his dark eyes and gave him a gentle smile. "I couldn't bear to part with it. I wore it all these years. Close to my heart. Surely that must tell you something."

He laughed shortly. "It must have given you a sense of triumph to have kept that all this time. To be honest, I'm surprised there's only one. In three years I would have expected you to add at least that many more."

Again Julie struggled to hide the pain. "No," she answered, lowering her gaze, "there was never anyone but you."

"You don't honestly expect me to believe that, do you?"

"It doesn't matter what you believe."

"Keep the ring around your neck. It represented a lot of devotion and feeling I don't have now. I'll buy another one later."

"If that's what you want," Julie whispered in defeat.

"I'll make the arrangements and get back to you with the details."

"Fine."

Julie didn't have to wait long to hear. Daniel phoned her the following afternoon with the information. The wedding was set for one week. Daniel picked her up after work Tuesday night so they could have the blood tests done and apply for the wedding license. After the required three-day wait, they would be married. Everything was cut-and-dried. Even as he relayed the details, Daniel had remained emotionless.

Julie's mother was shocked, but pleased, and planned to fly in for the wedding. Unfortunately Margaret Houser had to get back for volunteer work the next day. Julie was relieved that her mother's stay would be cut short. She wasn't sure how effectively she could act out the role of a happy bride.

The night before the wedding, with her mother sleeping in her bed, Julie tossed restlessly on the sofa. Just before dawn, she decided to give up on trying to sleep and moved from the couch. She doubted that she'd slept more than a couple of hours.

Standing at the window she stared into the night. The moon's silver rays fell upon the glistening dew of early morning.

Nervously she tugged at her lip. This was her wedding day and now in these last hours before the ceremony, her freedom was like sand silently slipping through her fingers. Nervous tension produced waves of nausea. Even now, Julie wasn't sure she was doing the right thing. Of one thing she was certain: right or wrong, she wouldn't walk out on Daniel a second time.

Several hours later, long after the last of the brilliant stars had faded with the morning sun, a car came to deliver Julie and her mother to the church. Clara Van Deen had insisted that her minister marry them. Julie had no objections and apparently Daniel didn't either.

Daniel met them at the church door. His eyes roamed over the white street-length dress Julie had chosen and something unreadable flickered across his face. Julie didn't know what he was thinking, and doubted that she really knew this man at all.

His casual "Are you ready?" stirred the gnawed sense she was making a terrible mistake. Swallowing, Julie decided to ignore it.

The ceremony was short. Daniel's steady voice responded to the minister's instructions as if the words held no meaning for him. In contrast, Julie's strained speech wobbled uncontrollably as she repeated her vows.

Daniel glanced at her when she pledged her love and a glint of challenge entered his gaze.

Her fingers trembled slightly as he slipped a plain gold band on her slim finger. The simplicity of the ring suited her, but she was sure Daniel had chosen something so plain as a contrast to the beautiful diamond he had given to her the first time. Julie was confident the contrast didn't stop there.

Julie's mother hugged them both, her eyes shining with happiness. All three rode to the hospital together and were allowed a short visit with Daniel's mother.

Clara Van Deen smiled as a tear of happiness slipped from the corner of her eye and dampened the pillowcase.

"Trust me, Julie," she whispered. "Things will work out."

Julie nodded, smiling feebly as she kissed the wrinkled brow.

From the hospital, Daniel and Julie drove her mother to the airport. Margaret Houser insisted on paying for everyone's lunch. If she noticed the stilted silence between the groom and bride, she said nothing.

Julie would have liked to visit longer with her mother. She yearned to hold onto her old life as long as possible, but Daniel was clearly in a hurry and after a few abrupt words, he ushered Julie back to the car.

Watching him as he drove, Julie's fingers clenched the small bouquet of flowers her mother had given her. The unfamiliar gold band felt strange against her finger and unconsciously she toyed with it, running it back and forth over her knuckle.

Stopped at a red light, Daniel caught her gazing at her hand. "Don't be so anxious to remove that wedding band. It's there for as long as I say. Understand?"

Julie tossed him an angry glare and murmured tightly, "Of course, I understand. You've made your feelings toward me and this marriage perfectly clear."

Neither spoke again until Daniel had parked. He owned a condominium in Wichita's most prestigious downtown area. The doorman smiled his welcome and held open the shiny glass door for Julie.

"Good afternoon, Mr. Van Deen," he said politely, his eyes widening with undisguised curiosity at the sight of Julie and the two suitcases Daniel carried.

Nodding curtly, Daniel placed his hand under Julie's elbow, hurrying her toward the elevator. The huge metal doors parted at the press of his finger and Julie was quickly ushered inside. The strained silence continued until he unlocked the door of the condominium, swinging it wide to allow Julie to enter first.

Reluctant to move inside, Julie hesitated, wondering what lay before her.

"Don't tell me you expect me to carry you over the threshold as well." The taunting arch of his brow brought a rush of embarrassed color to Julie's cheeks.

"No," she replied shortly and, with as much dignity as possible, entered her new life.

The condominium was surprisingly spacious. The tiled entryway led to a sunken living room carpeted in a plush brown pile. Two huge picture windows overlooked the downtown area and Julie paused to admire the fantastic view from fifteen floors up.

Pointedly, Daniel moved around her and briskly delivered her suitcase to what was apparently to be her bedroom. He stopped outside the door in the wide hallway.

"This is your room," he called abruptly, interrupting her search for familiar sights.

Julie lifted her eyes from the Century II Convention, Cultural Center, the Broadview Hotel and Holiday Inn Plaza and followed the sound of Daniel's voice to the hallway.

A glance inside the room confirmed her belief that this had been a guest room. Fitting, Julie realized, since she was little more than an unwelcome guest in Daniel's life.

"The rest of your things will be delivered sometime this afternoon," he informed her. "I have to get back to the office for a couple of hours."

Back to the office! Julie's mind shouted. They'd barely been married three hours. She'd taken the day off work. He could have at least done the same. They were in this marriage together.

"What am I supposed to do?" she asked mockingly in an attempt to hide her disappointment. "Make myself at home in a strange house, alone?"

"Unpack," he replied flippantly.

"That should take all of five minutes. What should I do then?"

"Don't tell me I have to stay home and baby-sit you for the next twenty years."

"No," Julie tossed out recklessly. "Go ahead and leave. There's no need to hurry back on my account."

Daniel's laugh was mirthless as he headed out the front door. "Don't worry."

Her calculation was correct. Five minutes later both suitcases were empty. After a quick inspection of the remainder of the condominium, Julie returned to her room. She yawned, raising her hands above her head and stretching. Her neck hurt from a sleepless night on the sofa. Slowly rotating her head, Julie hoped to ease the tightness from her tired muscles. She'd slept so little that she decided to take a nap. The bed yielded, soft and welcoming under her. Within minutes she fell into a deep, comfortable slumber.

Refreshed, she woke after four. Daniel had been gone a couple of hours. After leafing through a magazine, Julie toyed with the idea of going out for dinner and letting him come home to an empty apartment. It would serve him right. But, no, being antagonistic wouldn't help their situation. She pushed

the hair away from her temple and released a slow
breath. She would cook their meal and try to make the
best of things.

The compact kitchen was beautifully arranged and
well stocked. Apparently Daniel enjoyed cooking and
ate at home regularly or he had someone come in to
cook for him. Julie's hand tightened against the
counter. The thought of Daniel bringing another
woman into this kitchen produced an unaccustomed
feeling of jealousy. She'd managed to squelch those
uncomfortable sensations when he'd dated Sherry, but
now they washed over her, surprising Julie with their
intensity.

Working quickly, she prepared a fresh salad and
dessert, and then thawed two large steaks in the mi-
crowave until they were ready to grill.

She had the option of setting the dining room table
or the small area of the kitchen. After only a moment's deliberation she chose the dining room. This
was, after all, their wedding day, although Daniel
seemed to be doing his best to forget just that. If they
were going to build any kind of meaningful life, then
she would have to be the one to take the first step.

Another suitcase and several boxes from her apartment were delivered shortly after five and Julie spent
the next hour unpacking and arranging her things with
Daniel's. She wasn't surprised to find that they shared
similar tastes in literature and artwork. More than
once, as she placed her books on the shelf, she discovered that Daniel already had the same book.

Why the fact amazed her, Julie didn't know. They
had been surprisingly alike from their first meeting.

Fleetingly Julie wondered if Daniel still played tennis. It was on the courts that they'd first met. The attraction had been immediate and intense. They'd been so much in love.

As dusk fell over the city, Julie lit the candles, creating a warm, romantic mood. She regretted the harsh parting words with Daniel that afternoon. Maybe the dinner would show him that she was willing to work things out. She'd made the first step. But the next one had to come from Daniel.

Glancing at the table, she noted that the candle flames dancing against the illumination of city lights was breathtaking and alluringly poetic. Julie doubted that she would ever tire of looking at it.

The tiresome minutes ticked into drawn out hours and at eleven Julie accepted the fact that Daniel wouldn't be coming home for dinner. She didn't know if he'd be home at all. But if he walked in on the homey scene she'd created it would only amuse him.

After blowing out the candles and turning on the lights, she began to clear the table piece by piece, returning the china place settings to the rosewood cabinet.

When only half the dishes were cleared, the front door opened. Julie paused, her hand clenching the expensive plate tightly to her stomach, her heart pounding wildly.

From across the sizable room, Daniel's bold eyes held hers mesmerized.

Lowering her gaze, Julie offered him a nervous smile and resumed her task, praying he wouldn't comment. She should have known better.

"A romantic dinner complete with candlelight and the best dishes. What's this, Julie? An invitation to your bed?"

Chapter Five

No," she said, forcing her voice to sound light and carefree, "it wasn't that at all."

"Pity," he mumbled under his breath, but loud enough for her to hear.

Julie had to bite her tongue to keep from asking where he'd been. That was exactly what he wanted her to do, but she refused to play his games.

"If you'll excuse me, I think I'll go to bed."

Daniel remained standing in the tiled entryway, staring at her, his serious eyes searching her expression. "I didn't know if you'd eaten or not."

Averting her gaze, Julie shook her head. "No, I thought I'd wait for you."

"I'm surprised you did."

Wordlessly, Julie moved past him and down the hall to her room. Daniel had made it clear they wouldn't make the pretense of a honeymoon and she was scheduled to return to work in the morning. As she undressed, Julie could hear Daniel's movements in the kitchen.

Zipping up her housecoat, Julie moved across the hall to the bathroom to brush her teeth. The appealing aroma of broiling steak reminded her she hadn't eaten since early afternoon. Squaring her shoulders, she attacked her teeth with the brush. Not for anything would she go into that kitchen.

Back in her room, she sat on top of the bed and opened a recent best-seller. The light tap against the door shocked her.

"Your steak is ready." Daniel stuck his head in and smiled. "Medium rare, as I recall."

Julie opened her mouth to tell him exactly what he could do with the dinner, then abruptly stopped herself. It had been a tiring day for both of them and the last thing they needed was an argument to complicate matters.

"I'll be there in a minute." Feeling strangely pleased with the turn of events, Julie put on her slippers and joined him in the kitchen.

The table was set for two. Their steaks were served with grilled tomatoes and melted cheddar cheese on huge platters.

Smiling, Julie opened the refrigerator and brought out the crisp vegetable salad she'd made.

As she set the bowl on the table, Daniel commented nonchalantly, "There were some briefs I needed to review for a court case in the morning."

Julie paused as she sat at the table, her hand clenching the fork. Daniel was telling her why he was late. She hadn't expected it, confident he'd wanted her to fret. And she had.

"Perhaps it would be best if either one of us is going to be late to let the other know," she said evenly as the knife slid smoothly across the thick steak.

"Sounds fair," Daniel commented.

A soft smile touched her eyes as Julie continued eating. The evening had gotten off to an uneasy start, but they were working things out and that pleased her.

"We should probably make some other living arrangements," she suggested, forcing a conversational lightness to her voice.

"Like?"

"Since you did the cooking, I'll do the dishes."

"That sounds reasonable." His warm gaze touched her and Julie felt a weak sensation attack her stomach. Daniel hadn't smiled at her, really smiled, since she'd returned. She'd almost forgotten how potent one of his glances could be.

Julie continued to study him from beneath the thick lashes that veiled her eyes. Laying her knife across the curve of the plate, she looked up. "That was wonderful. I don't remember you being such an excellent cook."

"I've managed to pick up a few skills during the last couple of years," he murmured dryly.

Julie stood and carried their plates to the sink while Daniel poured them each a cup of coffee.

"Why don't we drink this in the living room?" he invited unexpectedly.

"I'll be there in a minute. I want to stick these things in the dishwasher."

When Julie joined him, Daniel was standing at the window looking out at the sparkling lights of the city.

"Mother seemed much improved today, didn't she?"

Julie took the coffee cup from the end table and sat down. "Yes, she did. There was some color in her cheeks for the first time since the attack."

"It's going to be a long uphill haul for her in the coming months."

"I know. I'll do anything possible to help her," Julie said and took a sip from the coffee cup. Daniel remained at the window with his back to her.

"I think we should agree that no matter what happens between us we won't take our squabbles to my mother."

"Of course not." Julie blinked. She was surprised that Daniel would think she'd run to his mother with every complaint. "If we need to talk something over, the person I'll come to is you," she said as matter-of-factly as possible.

"Good." He turned around and sat in the wing-backed chair beside her. "Don't worry about the housework. The cleaning lady comes in twice a week."

"What about the cooking?" Her hands cupped the mug as she avoided eye contact. "I hate to admit it, but I'm not much good in the kitchen. You're probably more adept at this cooking business than me. Do you want to take turns?"

"If you like."

"It might work out best for a while." She shrugged carelessly. How could they sit beside one another—man and wife—and talk of trivialities? Julie didn't want her marriage to begin with all these uncertainties gnawing at her. Twice before the wedding she'd tried to settle their past. Both times Daniel had abruptly cut her off. As much as possible he wanted to leave that time in their relationship behind them. Sadly the thought flashed through Julie's mind that they had no future until they faced the hurts and misunderstandings of the past. But tonight wasn't the time.

"You're looking thoughtful," Daniel commented.

"Sorry." She shook her head to clear her thoughts. "I guess I'm tired."

"I think I'll turn in too."

Together they carried their cups into the kitchen. Julie placed them in the dishwasher with the other dishes and Daniel showed her how to work it. The soft hum of running water followed them into the hallway.

He flipped off the light switch and the condominium went dark.

Julie's eyes adjusted quickly to the moonlit room.

"Can you find your way?"

"Sure," she murmured confidently. Their gazes met in the darkness and suddenly everything went still. Daniel's look held her motionless. She couldn't see his eyes well enough to know what he was thinking. How long they stood there not speaking, Julie didn't know. It seemed an eternity.

When his hand reached out and caressed her cheek, a warming sensation spread down her neck. Releasing a soft sigh, she closed her eyes and placed her hand over his.

"Good night, Julie," he said tenderly and removed his hand. He walked her to her room and hesitated long enough in the open doorway for her heartbeat to quicken.

Their eyes met and for a fleeting moment the hurt that had driven them apart all but faded. Unconsciously, Julie took a wishful step in his direction. This man was her husband. They were meant to be together.

"If you'd like, I'll cook breakfast in the morning," she offered, wanting an excuse to linger with him in the darkness even if it meant asking inane questions.

He didn't answer for so long that Julie wondered if he'd heard her speak. "I thought you said you weren't much of a cook."

"I can manage breakfast."

"Did you dine out so often?"

The question caught her completely off guard. "I don't understand."

He raised his voice with tight impatience. "Is the reason you can't cook because you dated so much?"

"No," she answered simply. "I hardly went out at all." She couldn't when she'd left her heart with him.

Silvery moonlight filled the narrow hallway as Julie intently studied her husband, waiting for a reaction.

"I wish I could believe that," he said with a sigh, "but you're much too beautiful not to have men fawning over you." Abruptly he turned away.

The alarm on the clock radio went off at six, filling the silent room with instant music. Julie lay in bed several minutes, listening to a couple of songs before throwing back the covers and climbing out of bed.

Slipping into her housecoat, she ambled into the kitchen, yawning as she put on a pot of coffee. Already the morning was glorious. The sun was shining and Julie stood at the window looking down on the city as it stirred to life.

When she turned around, she found Daniel standing at the coffeepot waiting for enough liquid to drain through so he could have a cup.

"Good morning," she greeted him with a warm smile.

Daniel mumbled something unintelligible under his breath.

"Did you say something?" she asked as she took the empty cup out of his hand, and poured what little coffee had drained through into his mug.

"No," he grumbled.

"No one told me you were such a grouch in the mornings," she teased.

"Do you have to smile so brightly?"

"No," she said, laughing softly. "I'll go get dressed and stay out of your way until you're civil."

"That's probably a good idea."

Humming, Julie returned to her bedroom and dressed. The outfit she chose was a new one, a two-piece gray-and-blue striped dress with a wide vee neckline. In normal circumstances she probably wouldn't have chosen the dress for work, but she considered her choice a means of wooing her husband.

Slipping the pumps on her feet, she completed the final touches to her makeup and hair before entering the kitchen.

The bacon was sizzling in the pan when Daniel came in and poured himself a second cup of coffee.

"How do you want your eggs? Over easy?" She turned and was surprised to see the scowl that twisted his mouth in disapproval.

"Is something wrong?"

"That dress."

"It's new. Don't you like it?" She swallowed tightly. Julie hadn't needed a saleslady to tell her the outfit was becoming on her. The blue tones matched the color of her eyes perfectly.

"It's a little revealing, don't you think?"

"Revealing?" Julie gasped. "Where?"

Daniel picked up the morning paper and sat down. "The neckline."

"The neckline?" Julie's hand flew to the V-shaped front. She'd always dressed modestly and there was nothing about this outfit or anything else she owned that could be considered less than proper. "There's nothing wrong with this dress," she replied in even tones.

"That's a matter of opinion," he returned from behind the open newspaper.

"How do you want your eggs?" Julie repeated her question, fighting back her impatience.

The newspaper didn't move, effectively blocking her out. "I've lost my appetite."

"So have I," she whispered brokenly and turned off the burner.

The drive to the office took only a few minutes. Neither spoke. Julie's hands were clenched in her lap like a schoolchild, her head held rigid with her eyes focused straight ahead. She hadn't changed clothes, nor would she. Daniel was being unreasonable. A wry smile touched her mouth. And she'd anticipated gently courting him with the new dress.

Daniel pulled into a parking garage across the street and into the allotted space.

"I may be late tonight."

Julie answered without looking at him. "I thought I'd go to the hospital after work."

"Then I'll meet you there."

They sounded like robots, their voices clipped and emotionless.

Sherry was at her desk when Julie walked in the office. Julie paused and did a double take.

"Is that really you, Sherry?" she joked as she closed the door. "Or are my eyes playing tricks on me again? Sherry early? That's impossible."

The returning smile was weak and wavering. "Morning." She lowered her head and blew her nose in a tissue. "I guess it's a shock to see me, isn't it?" The soft voice faltered slightly.

"Sherry, what's wrong?"

"Wrong?" She laughed. "What makes you think something's wrong?"

"Maybe it's the mountain of wet tissues, or the red eyes and weak smile. But then I've always had the reputation of being a good sleuth."

Sherry made a gallant effort at smiling. She gestured weakly, waving the palm of her hand.

Julie had worried something like this would happen when Sherry learned she'd married Daniel.

"I guess I should have said something the first time you mentioned Daniel," Julie murmured apologetically. "I wouldn't want to hurt you, Sherry, not for anything. Daniel and I have known each other for several years."

Sherry glanced up with a blank look. "What are you talking about?"

"Daniel and me. I should have explained that we've known each other for several years."

"I didn't think either of you were crazy enough to get married after a two-week courtship. That sounds like something I'd do. But not you and Daniel."

"Then why the tears and the dismal look?"

"Andy." Sherry's voice wobbled.

"Your ex-husband?"

Sherry tugged another Kleenex from the brightly colored box and nodded. "The divorce isn't final until the end of the month."

"Second thoughts?" Julie only knew a little about Sherry's marriage from the bits of information her friend had let drop a couple of times. They didn't have any real reason to separate. Both had been overly involved in their jobs. They'd grown apart and apparently out of love. The trial separation had led to the decision to file for the divorce. In the short time Julie had known her co-worker it hadn't been difficult to recognize that Sherry had set out to prove how much fun she could have without her husband.

"I . . . I saw Andy last night."

"Did you get a chance to talk?" Julie questioned softly. She didn't want to pry but thought that Sherry might feel better if she confided in someone.

"Talk!" She hiccuped loudly. "There was a voluptuous blonde draped all over him."

"But Sherry, that shouldn't bother you. For heaven's sake, you've gone out a dozen times with as many different men just since I've known you."

"Yes, but that was different."

"How?"

"Andy didn't care if I saw someone else."

"How can you be so sure?" Julie interjected the question. "Maybe he cares very much. Maybe he's decided the time has come for him to start dating again too."

"Not Andy. He's always hated blondes."

"You're blond," Julie chided.

"I know, but the type of woman he was with last night isn't like anyone that would interest him." Sherry wiped the moisture from her cheeks and inhaled slowly. "There's irony in this whole thing. I'd set my sights on Danny, convinced that he was the perfect man for me...and he's another Andy. They're so much alike it's ridiculous. How could I have been so blind—" she paused to take in a deep breath "—and stupid?"

"I've done some stupid things in my life," Julie admitted with a wry smile.

Their boss, Mr. Barrett, came into the room and absently nodded his greeting as he hung his coat in the closet. He seemed about to say something when he noticed Sherry's red face. Swiftly he retreated into his office, closing the door. With a grin, Julie said, "Why don't we see if we can take lunch together and talk some more."

"I'd like that."

The phone rang and Julie pushed down the button to take the call.

Ten minutes later, Julie replaced the phone and took the top file from her In basket.

"I meant to tell you earlier how nice you look today. Is that a new outfit?"

"Yes." Julie's head snapped up. "Do you like it?"

"It's perfect for you."

"What about the neckline?" She tilted her head up and arched her shoulders.

"What about it?"

"It's not too revealing?"

"Revealing?" Sherry echoed. "No way."

"That's what I thought," she mumbled and turned back to the file.

Clara Van Deen attempted to smile when Julie entered the intensive care unit that afternoon. She lifted her hand to Julie, who clasped it between hers.

"How's my new daughter?"

"How's my new mother?"

Clara closed her eyes and when she opened them again they were glistening with unshed tears. "Better now that I'm assured I've made up for some of the pain I've caused you and Daniel."

"I love him," Julie admitted gently. "I came back because of my love for him."

"And Daniel loves you. Don't ever doubt that, Julie. Though I know little of his life anymore, I realize he saw lots of women. But, Julie, there was never anyone he truly loved. No one but you."

Gently, Julie squeezed the old woman's hand. "I'll make him a good wife."

"I don't doubt for a minute that you will." The returning smile was weak but infinitely happy.

Daniel arrived thirty minutes later. Julie was in the waiting room leafing through a dog-eared magazine she'd already read through twice. She glanced up expectantly when he entered the area.

Daniel's gaze dwelled on her neckline and the fullness of her breasts. A closed expression masked his features.

"Your mother's looking very good," Julie said softly.

Daniel nodded abruptly. "I'll spend some time with her and then we'll leave."

Of their own volition Julie's eyes were drawn to her husband. His rugged appeal gave the impression that he worked out of doors. His face was tanned for early spring and Julie suspected he had continued to play tennis although he hadn't mentioned it. But then they hadn't talked about a lot of things. The sensuous mouth was compressed into a tight line.

"I talked to the doctor this afternoon," Daniel announced casually and rubbed his hand along the back of his neck as he paced the waiting room.

"And?" Julie set the magazine aside and uncrossed her legs.

"He said mother's improving enough for him to consider doing the open-heart surgery."

"When?" Julie asked and breathed in deeply.

"A month from now, maybe longer."

"That's wonderful news." If the surgery was a success the possibility of Daniel's mother returning to a normal life would be greatly increased.

"Is it?" Daniel returned almost flippantly. "If she gains enough strength to make it to surgery her chances are only fifty-fifty she'll survive the ordeal."

"But what are they without it?"

He stalked to the far side of the room and pivoted sharply. "Far less than that."

"Is there a choice?" She could understand and shared his concern, but the chance of a longer, healthier life for his mother was worth the risk. Daniel, however, didn't look nearly as confident. "Everything's going to be fine."

"How do you know that?"

"I don't," Julie admitted, "but your mother's content, her spirits are good and she has the will to live. Her attitude is positive and that's bound to help." It was on the tip of her tongue to tell Daniel that on the day Clara had taken ill, she'd mentioned to Julie how she longed to hold her grandchildren. Julie knew sheer willpower would see her mother-in-law through this surgery.

Daniel's expression tightened as he studied her.

The nurse arrived and directed him into the intensive care area. Julie stayed behind since the staff preferred that their patients have only one visitor at a time.

As they drove home Julie noticed that a spark of amusement seemed to flicker in and out of Daniel's eyes.

"What's so funny?" she asked him later as she set the table for dinner.

"What makes you think something's amusing?"

Julie pretended an interest in the fresh green salad she was tossing. "Every time I look up it seems you're trying to keep from laughing."

"Something mother said, that's all." He didn't elaborate.

"About me?" she asked stiffly, disliking the fact she could have been the brunt of their joke.

"Indirectly."

They ate in almost total silence. Not an intended silence, at least not on Julie's part. They were married but shared nothing in common as yet. Daniel hadn't allowed her into his life. Julie was confident that the sharing would come with time. The one thing they desperately needed to talk about, Daniel refused to discuss.

"Do you still play tennis?" Julie asked as she cleared the small table, hoping that he'd follow through with her question and suggest that they play again.

"Often enough."

Julie noticed that he didn't ask if she still played. They'd met on the courts and had been a popular doubles team. Julie still enjoyed the game, but didn't know how to volunteer the information without making it look as if she was looking for an invitation, which she was.

"I'll do the dishes later." Daniel broke into her un-happy thoughts. "There are a few papers I want to go over tonight."

"Do you bring work home often?" Julie hadn't meant the question derogatorily, but the look Daniel flashed her showed his disapproval.

"Hardly at all."

"I'll do the dishes," she volunteered.

"No," he said abruptly. "When I say I'm going to do something, I do it."

Julie gripped the edge of the oak table and ex-haled. "In other words you don't walk out five days before the wedding. That's what you're saying isn't it, Daniel?"

"That's exactly what I'm saying," he said in steel-sharp tones.

In a haze of pain, Julie stood and scooted her chair to the table. Soundlessly she moved out of the kitchen, reached for a sweater and headed for the front door.

"Where are you going?" Daniel demanded.

"Out," she replied with a saccharine sweet smile and closed the door behind her. Half hoping Daniel would come after her, Julie lingered in the hall out-side the condominium. She should have known bet-ter.

Without her purse and nowhere to go, Julie was back within an hour, having done nothing more than take a brisk walk.

When she returned to the condo, Daniel was in his den, or at least she assumed he was. The two pans from their meal were washed and stacked on the kitchen counter. Julie dried them and put them away.

When she'd finished she glanced up to note that Daniel was standing in the open doorway of the den watching her.

"So you came back."

"What's the matter," she said flippantly, "were you hoping I wouldn't?"

A muscle twitched in his jaw and the pencil in his hands snapped in two. He pivoted and returned to his den.

Julie closed her eyes and took in several calming breaths. This grueling tension between them was fast taking its toll. She hated any kind of discord. At eighteen she'd avoided confrontations and had paid dearly for her mistake. She wasn't the same Julie she had been then. She didn't avoid conflict these days, but she didn't wish to instigate it either.

Daniel remained in his den, the door closed, while Julie sat alone in the living room reading. Although her eyelashes fluttered closed more than once, she shook herself awake, determined to be up when Daniel came out. She wasn't going to run away, not anymore. It was important that he recognize that.

Again and again her eyelids drooped closed until Julie gave up the effort and closed her book. Flipping the light switch to its lowest setting, she leaned her head against the back of the chair to rest her eyes and obediently surrendered to the welcoming tide of slumber.

"Julie." Daniel's whisper woke her. "You'll get a crick in your neck."

Her blue eyes opened slowly and she straightened. The soft glow from the lamp was the only light in the house. Daniel stood above her, his shirt open to reveal the mat of hair on his chest. He studied her and time seemed to come to a halt. Julie felt herself drowning in the tender look in her husband's eyes. She yearned to reach out to him, slip her arms around his neck and gently place her mouth over his. He hadn't kissed her, had avoided touching her, and Julie felt if he turned and walked away from her now she'd die.

"Julie." Her name came on a tormented whisper as he brushed a long strand of hair from her temple.

She knew the look in her eyes must have revealed the hunger she felt for his touch. The desperate need she had to be loved, forgiven and trusted again.

He helped her stand, his touch almost impersonal.

"Daniel," she pleaded softly, wanting to cry with frustration.

Without a word he slipped his arms around her, his dark gaze feasting on her softly parted lips as he slowly, silently, eliminated the distance between them.

Julie released a trembling sigh as she slid her hands over his shoulders and linked her fingers at the base of his neck. "Oh, Daniel," she whispered, "I've waited so long."

He crushed her to his chest, his mouth moving sweetly over hers as he arched her closer.

Mindlessly, Julie obeyed as he kissed her again and again. She thrilled to the urgency of his mouth as if he couldn't receive enough. As if she couldn't give enough. When he buried his face against the curve of her neck, Julie smiled contentedly, while her hands sought his thick hair.

Daniel straightened and looked into her eyes. Smiling, Julie brushed her mouth over his and kissed the tiny cleft in his chin. The very spot she'd loved to tease with her tongue all those years ago. She wanted him to know she hadn't forgotten, not anything.

He stiffened against her and abruptly tugged his arms free. "Good night, Julie," he murmured stiffly before turning and walking away. He was telling her he hadn't forgotten anything, either.

For one unbearable moment, Julie didn't breathe. How many times would he walk away from her to make up for the one time she'd left him? How many hurts must she suffer to compensate for the damage she had inflicted against his male pride? Standing alone in the darkened room, Julie could find no answers. Slowly she turned and went into her room, hoping to find some peace in sleep.

The next day was almost identical to the one before. Silently, they rode to work together. From work they went to the hospital, taking turns visiting his mother. Daniel cooked dinner while she changed clothes.

"I'm going to the library," she announced as she placed their plates in the dishwasher.

"How long will you be?" Daniel asked without looking up from the mail.

"An hour." Anything was better than sitting in a silent house again while Daniel closed himself off from her in his den.

He shrugged as if what she did was of little concern to him.

Julie hesitated. "Would you like to come?"

"I've got things to do around here."

Julie let herself out the front door, her heart aching. The first night she'd accused Daniel of playing games. Now she was the one escaping, hoping that he'd say something to prove that he wanted her to stay. He didn't.

Chapter Six

Saturday morning Daniel left the condominium before Julie climbed out of bed. Lying awake with her bedroom door partially open, Julie listened to his hushed movements as he walked down the hall. She expected him to go into the kitchen and was mildly surprised to hear the front door click a few moments later.

Carelessly tossing back the covers, she slipped out of bed and found a pot of coffee and a note on the kitchen counter top. The message read: *Playing tennis all day.*

All day, Julie mused resentfully. They'd talked about the game earlier in the week. There had been ample opportunity for him to have included her in today's outing had he wished...which he obviously hadn't.

After brewing a fresh pot of coffee, Julie sat at the round oak table, her palms cupping the mug. An abundance of pride tilted her chin at a sharp, upward angle. She'd known when she agreed to marry Daniel that there were several factors working against them. Some days Julie was convinced that Daniel would never forgive nor forget the hurt she'd inflicted on him by leaving. Then at other times, odd moments when he didn't think she'd noticed, she could feel his gaze studying her. Daniel had been unable to disguise the tender look fast enough. He hadn't kissed her or touched her since that one night. Julie recognized he regretted that one slip and had taken measures to ensure that it wouldn't happen again.

Restless, she killed time by cooking a light breakfast, then dressed casually in washed-out jeans and a plain sweatshirt. The last of her things had been moved from the apartment. Almost everything had been unpacked and what remained needed to be placed in storage. Only a few of her everyday items were necessary since Daniel's condominium was fully furnished.

Stacking the cardboard crates in the bottom of her closet, Julie located the box that was filled with mementos of her courtship with Daniel. Now that they were married, she could set them out freely. If she placed their engagement photo in full view it might prompt him to discuss the very things he chose to ignore.

Encouraged at the thought, she set the gold-framed picture on top of the television and stepped back to examine it. As always, her heart constricted at the bright hope and promise that shone from their eyes. Daniel's appearance had altered over the years, but Julie vowed that in time all that would change and the special light of his love for her would again shine.

She placed a few other items here and there and then stood in the middle of the room, hands on her hips, to admire her efforts. The condominium, bit by bit, reflected a part of them as a loving, happy couple. Daniel couldn't help but be affected by it. Undoubtedly he would be surprised that she'd kept those things, but she wanted him to understand that although she'd left Wichita, she'd never forgotten him nor stopped loving him.

After a hot shower, Julie had lunch and decided to stop in at the hospital and visit her mother-in-law.

The older woman turned her face toward Julie as she entered the intensive care unit.

"Good afternoon," Julie said with a warm smile and lightly brushed her lips across Clara's cheek. "How are you feeling today?"

"Much better."

She looked improved and Julie felt encouraged.

"Where's Daniel?" Clara wanted to know.

"He's playing tennis." Silently Julie hoped that her mother-in-law wouldn't ask for any more details because she wouldn't know what to tell the older woman. As much as possible, Julie hoped to paint an optimistic picture of their marriage, but she was unwilling to lie.

"That's right," Mrs. Van Deen murmured and smiled softly, "Daniel mentioned something about playing in a tournament this weekend. I'm surprised you aren't at the Country Club with him. As I recall, you two made an excellent doubles team.''

So he'd told his mother and hadn't bothered to mention it to her. Maybe he had another partner and didn't want Julie interfering with his prearranged plans. The thought produced a flicker of jealous anger. Quickly she squashed it before her mother-in-law could read her expression.

"Julie, you still play, don't you?''

"I'm a bit rusty,'' she claimed with a feeble effort at smiling. The Country Club; Julie could vividly recall how uncomfortable she'd been around those people. Daniel had taken her there several times to dinner or for a set of tennis, but Julie had been unable to overcome her feelings of inferiority.

"I thought you'd want to be with him,'' Clara continued, studying Julie.

"I came to give you our love before meeting Daniel later.'' Julie told the white lie uneasily. But she would show up at the Country Club. The time had come for her to face some of the other insecurities of the past.

"There's no need to disrupt your day coming to visit me,'' Clara said with a tired sigh. "I already know how much you care about me. If I live or die is of no consequence to me. All I want before I go is the assurance that the two of you are happy.'' The white-haired woman regarded Julie seriously. "I wouldn't, however, be upset to hold a grandchild or two.'' She paused and attempted a smile. "Daniel seemed quite amused when I mentioned how much I was looking forward to grandchildren.''

So that was what he'd been so smug about the other night. "I think he feels we should wait," Julie improvised quickly.

"His words exactly. But try to convince him, Julie. I don't have all the time in the world. And he's at the age when he should be thinking of starting a family."

Gently, Julie brushed the hair from Clara's face. "I'll mention it," she promised. "But remember we've only been married a short while."

The tired eyes fluttered closed. "It seems so much longer. In my muddled mind I find it difficult to remember you were gone all those years."

"My heart was here," Julie said softly.

"Would you read to me, dear?" she asked. "My eyes are so weak."

"I'd be happy to."

Although her thoughts were troubled, Julie read until she was certain Clara was asleep, then she quietly slipped from the room. Her mind was set on facing Daniel at the Country Club, but her determination wavered. Her unexpected arrival could be uncomfortable for everyone involved. No, she reasoned. As his wife she had the right to go and watch her husband. Resolutely, she left the hospital, got into her car and headed for the outskirts of town.

Julie was lucky to find a parking place in the crowded lot. The tennis courts and surrounding areas were jammed with spectators. Julie signed in as Daniel's wife and was grateful no one questioned her.

It only took her a few minutes to find her husband. He was on the courts in what she learned was the semifinal singles match. There was a space for her in the bleachers, and she sat there silently engrossed in the competition. A feeling of pride filled her when Daniel won the match. The championship game was played fifteen minutes later. Julie clenched her fists several times at tense moments. Daniel's composure astonished her. He lost the title, but shook hands with his opponent and came off the court joking and smiling.

The crowd gathered around the winner as the stands emptied. Julie made her way to her husband.

Daniel was wiping his face with a hand towel.

"Nice game," she said from behind him.

He didn't pause or give any indication he was surprised as he turned toward her. "How'd you know where to find me?" His look revealed little.

"Your mother mentioned the tournament, so I thought I'd stop by and cheer you on." She offered him a fabricated smile.

"I saw you take a seat in the stands."

"You were good." She noticed that he didn't indicate one way or another how he felt about her unexpected arrival. "Your game's improved."

"I've played better." He made busywork of packing away his racket.

"Good game, Van Deen," a deep baritone voice intoned from behind them.

Julie sensed Daniel stiffen. "Thanks." Casually he looped the towel around his neck.

Julie didn't recognize the tall, athletic man who had joined them.

"I see you've brought your own cheering section along."

Daniel slipped his hands around Julie's waist, bringing her to his side. "Patterson, meet my wife, Julie. Julie, this is my friend and associate, Jim Patterson."

"Your wife!" he echoed. "When did all this happen?"

"Recently."

Jim chuckled and rubbed the side of his jaw in a bemused action. "It had to have been recent. Real recent. Does Kali know?"

At the mention of the other woman's name, Julie eyed her husband speculatively. She had wondered before their wedding if there was another woman Daniel was seeing seriously and at the time had doubted it. Sherry would have known if he'd been romantically involved with someone else. But it was obvious Jim knew more than her co-worker.

"I haven't talked to Kali yet," Daniel replied stiffly.

"This calls for a celebration," Jim said hurriedly, trying to cover the awkward moment. "Let me buy you two a drink."

"Not today," Daniel answered for them. "Unfortunately, Julie has an appointment and must leave." His arm slid possessively from her waist to the back of her neck. "I'll see you to your car, honey." His hand tightened as he steered her toward the parking area.

"It's a pleasure to have met you . . . Patterson." Julie twisted her head to look back.

"We'll have that drink another time," Jim promised with a brief salute.

Once they were free of spectators, Julie pushed Daniel's hand loose. "What was that all about? And who is Kali?'' She was so frustrated she could hardly speak.

A muscle leaped in his determined jaw. "No one who need concern you."

"And why couldn't we have stayed for a drink?" she sputtered out breathlessly. "It's time I met your friends. I'm your wife."

"Don't remind me."

His words couldn't have hurt more had he reached out and physically slapped her. Tears brimmed from the depths of her eyes, threatening to crash over the thick wall of her lashes. She inhaled sharply and refused to give him the satisfaction of seeing her tears.

Daniel rammed his hands into his pockets and looked as if he was about to say something more, but Julie didn't wait to find out. Pride dictating her actions, she briskly turned and walked away. She couldn't get out of the parking lot fast enough.

Unwilling to return to the empty condominium, she drove around until the hurt and anger had dissipated enough for her to think clearly. So there'd been another woman. All right, she could accept that as long as this Kali remained in the past. She'd need to be told soon, however, that Daniel had married or it could cause awkward moments in the future.

Julie released a ragged breath. She was adult enough to realize that Daniel hadn't buried his head in the sand during the years she was gone. It would be unreasonable to expect anything less, but it hurt more than she thought possible. What worried her more was his determination not to tell her about Kali.

When she arrived home two hours later, Daniel was restlessly pacing the living room carpet.

"Julie." He stopped and walked a couple of steps toward her before pausing and jerking a hand through his hair. "Where were you?"

"I went for a drive. I needed time to think a few things through."

He scowled and nodded.

She glanced at her watch. "I didn't realize it was so late. It's my turn to cook isn't it?" she continued, chattering nervously. "I'll put something on right away. You must be starved."

The sound of his voice followed her as she headed for the kitchen. "I thought I'd take you out tonight."

"Take me out?"

"As you said earlier, it's time you and I were seen together."

Julie inhaled a quivering breath of pleasure. The dinner invitation was his way of telling her he was sorry for what had happened that afternoon. It wasn't an eloquent apology, but one that encouraged her immeasurably.

"Well?" Hands buried deep in his pockets, he studied her.

She replied with a slow, sensual smile. "I'd like that."

"Wear something fancy."

The soft smile faltered. "I'm afraid I may not have anything appropriate. Would you mind if we went someplace less formal?" she asked him stiffly.

"Why? As I recall, you liked the party scene."

"I was nineteen years old and incredibly stupid," she told him in a shaky voice. "I never liked any of it, but I couldn't tell you that. I was afraid if you knew how shy I really was, you wouldn't want me."

A flicker of surprise touched Daniel's rugged features. "Our relationship seems riddled with misunderstandings, doesn't it? Why didn't you tell me how you felt?"

"I was so crazy about you, I was ready to become anything you wanted."

"Everything but my wife," he said, his expression impassive, almost stoic.

"I couldn't," she cried. "Not then." She left the kitchen and moved into her bedroom. Leaning against the door, she closed her eyes. Surely Daniel must realize that if they'd gone through with the wedding three years ago their marriage would have been doomed. Sighing unevenly, Julie recognized that their union wasn't any more secure now. The thought saddened her.

Swallowing down the hurts that crowded in around her, Julie changed into a pale blue dress with a matching white jacket. A glance in the mirror confirmed that even the most critical eye would find no fault with the neckline. White high-heeled sandals graced her feet while a single strand of pearls hung elegantly around her throat. Daniel had given her the pearls, but she doubted that he would remember that. He'd given her so many beautiful things.

She moved into the living room, where her husband was waiting. He wore dark poplin slacks with a color-coordinated shirt under a sports coat.

The atmosphere was congenial as he pulled out of the parking garage. "I made a phone call and was able to get last minute tickets for the dinner theater."

Julie nodded agreeably. "That sounds wonderful. What's playing?"

His mouth twisted wryly. "*Never Too Late*," he said and cast an amused glance at Julie.

"Seems appropriate," she murmured as she returned his smile. Deep within herself she prayed that it wasn't too late for them.

When his hand reached for hers, Julie felt a shimmering warmth skid up her arm from his touch. It had always been like that. Daniel was capable of stirring sensations in her she had only dreamed existed. Never would she be able to respond like this to another man.

The dinner was wonderful and the comedy had both of them amused and laughing. At least for those few hours, they set aside their difficulties and were man and wife without the past intruding.

"Would you like to go someplace for a drink?" Daniel asked on their way out of the Crown Uptown Dinner Theater.

"We could if you like," she agreed, "but I think I'd prefer a hot cup of coffee in our own kitchen so I can prop up my feet. I should have known better than to wear tight shoes."

"If you promise to be sensible the next time I take you to dinner, then I'll rub them for you." Daniel admonished with a lazy smile.

"You're on." It felt so good to joke with him. Tonight it was so easy to pretend that they were exactly as they appeared to be: a loving husband and wife enjoying an evening out together.

While Julie made them a cup of cappuccino, Daniel turned on the stereo. Mellow music filled the condominium, a love ballad so beautiful that for a moment Julie was lost in the meaningful words.

She carried the cups into the living room and sat on the opposite end of the sofa from her husband. "Here." She swung her feet onto his lap, "Do your magic."

While she sipped from the tiny cup of creamy coffee, Daniel gently massaged her feet, rubbing the aches until she sighed with pleasure.

"Why do you wear those silly things? You've got a blister on your heel."

"I know," she muttered, "but they're the only decent pair of dress shoes I have."

"Is that a hint for me to buy you a new wardrobe?"

Julie went completely still. She swung her feet onto the floor. "No," she answered evenly. It was difficult to infer from his tone of voice if he was teasing or sincere. She studied his face, but any telling emotion was hidden behind a noncommittal expression.

"A husband enjoys buying his wife gifts. You certainly had no difficulty accepting things from me in the past. You've kept them too, if the pearls are an indication."

"I kept every part of you I could," she whispered through the uncertainty. Her gaze fell on the television and she stiffened with bewilderment. The framed engagement picture was missing. Her eyes shot to the bookcase, thinking he may have moved it.

"What happened to the picture?" She rolled to her bare feet. "I put it here this morning and now it's gone."

"I put it away."

"Away?" she echoed in disbelief. "What do you mean by away?"

Daniel stood and stalked to the opposite side of the living room. "It's in your bedroom."

"But why?" she cried again, watching his reaction. She felt unbelievably hurt.

"Because I was angry and took it out on the photo." Julie went pale. "You...didn't destroy it, did you?"

"No, but I was tempted. I don't want anything around to remind me of that time in my life."

"I see," she said and breathed heavily, fighting off the pain that came at her in waves. She refused to give in to the tears. For a minute she thought she glimpsed pain in his eyes. But he didn't answer her. Instead he walked into his den and closed the door.

Julie was shaking so badly that the cappuccino sloshed over the rim of the cup and into the saucer as she carried it into the kitchen. After rinsing out the cups she returned to the living room and removed the other mementos she'd placed there. Those items, however small, meant a great deal to her. She couldn't bear to have Daniel reject them as he had the photograph.

Her sleep was troubled. She woke from a fitful slumber at three, her heart heavy. Just when it looked like she was making some progress with Daniel, something would happen and she'd realize how far they had to go.

Slipping from the bed, she wandered into the kitchen and poured herself a glass of milk. She stood at the picture window, looking down on the silent, sleeping city below. She sensed, more than heard Daniel come up behind her. Not moving, Julie remained as she was.

"You couldn't sleep?"

"No." The one word tumbled from her throat as the tears filled and shimmered in her eyes.

Gently, his hand clasped her shoulders and he pressed his face into her hair. "Julie, I'm sorry about the picture. The minute I saw how much it meant to you I regretted taking it down. To be honest, I wasn't sure why you put it out. I thought you wanted to torment me." His fingers smoothed the dark hair from her temple.

"Torment you?" Abruptly, she turned, her eyes seeking his in the moonlight. Dark, dancing shadows flickered against the opposite wall, making it impossible to read his expression.

He took the glass of milk from her hand and set it aside. With an infinite tenderness he brought her into the warm circle of his arms. His chin rested against the top of her head as his hands roamed up and down her back in a massaging, rotating motion.

How long he held her, Julie didn't know. It felt so right to be in his arms again. In some ways it was as if she'd never left.

A finger under her chin lifted her mouth to his. Her response was automatic. Julie stood on tiptoes and fit her body to his, feeling Daniel resist momentarily as she melted against him.

"I'm sorry, Julie," he whispered on a husky note and relaxed, kissing her again.

"I know," she whispered and tantalizingly brushed her lips over his. Daniel moaned and hungrily claimed her mouth, holding her so close it was difficult to breathe.

"I won't make you cry again," he promised as his fingers smoothed the dark hair from her temple. His eyes were shining into hers and Julie sighed longingly and pressed her face to his shoulder. Nestled in the comfort of his embrace, she tried unsuccessfully to stifle a yawn.

"Come on, sleepyhead," he whispered and kissed the top of her head. "I'll tuck you in." With arms around each other's waists, Daniel led her back to the bedroom. Her heart thundered in her breast as he helped her into the bed and stood above her. He wanted her, Julie was sure of it. She was his wife and he longed to take her in his arms and love her as a husband. Yet he stood as he was, his face revealing the battle he waged within himself.

"Good night," he whispered finally, turning away.

"Good night," she repeated, struggling to disguise her own frustration. He lingered in the doorway and Julie's heart was beating like a locomotive. She sat up, using her elbows for leverage. "Daniel?"

"Yes?" He turned back eagerly.

"Thank you for tonight. I enjoyed the show."

"I did too," he said softly. "We'll do it again soon." He hesitated. "Next time I'll take you to Gatsby's."

"Really?"

"If you'd like we could take up tennis again."

"I'd like that," she responded happily, "very much."

"Tomorrow?"

"All right, if you want."

To his credit, Daniel did play a set of tennis with her the following morning. But he repeatedly glanced at his wristwatch, obviously not enjoying their match. He beat her easily, but then it had been a long time since Julie had played anyone who challenged her the way Daniel did. He seemed uncommunicative and out of sorts by the time they finished. It would have been better not to have played at all. She couldn't understand his attitude. And part of the reason she wanted to play was so she could meet his friends. Daniel introduced her to no one.

"Half the morning's gone," he commented on their way off the courts. Again he glanced at his watch impatiently. "I've got several things that need to be done this afternoon."

Julie remained tight-lipped as they returned to the condominium. He'd been the one to suggest the game, not her. Almost immediately Daniel closed himself in his den. When lunch was ready a half hour later, Julie went into his room to find him poring over books and papers. He barely noticed that she was there.

"Would you prefer to eat in here or in the kitchen?"

Daniel glanced up surprised. "Here."

Julie brought in a tray with tomato soup and two grilled cheese sandwiches.

"Thanks," he muttered.

Julie ate a silent meal while leafing through the thick Sunday paper. Later in the afternoon she did the weekly shopping and a few other errands. On her way back to the condominium, Julie stopped off at the hospital. Clara Van Deen was being transferred out of intensive care the next morning and Julie promised to stop in for a visit on her way home from work the following evening.

On the return trip home, Julie picked up hamburgers at a drive-in for their dinner. To her surprise, Daniel remained in his den. "You're still at it?"

He looked up and nodded. "This case is more involved than I thought."

"I brought you some dinner."

"Good, I can use a break. What'd you make?"

Julie glanced at him guiltily. "Well, I didn't exactly cook anything. I brought hamburgers home."

"Julie," Daniel groaned. "Sometime in the next twenty years, you're going to have to think about learning to cook."

In twenty years, she mused contentedly, they'd still be together and she'd do exactly that.

Chapter Seven

"Married life doesn't seem to agree with you," Sherry commented, watching Julie work.

"What do you mean?" Julie knew she wasn't doing a good job of hiding her feelings. Another week had passed and just when she thought the tension was lessening between her and Daniel something would happen to set them back. They hardly spoke in the mornings. Even during the drive downtown he was strangely quiet, preoccupied. In the evenings they visited his mother, came home and ate dinner. Almost immediately afterward, he'd hole himself up in his den. Sometimes Julie wondered if he was aware of her at all. He treated her more like a roommate than a wife. She didn't know when he slept. He seemed to be avoiding her as much as possible.

"Maybe I should keep my mouth shut," Sherry continued, "but you don't have the look of a happy bride."

Julie bit into her trembling bottom lip as she opened a file and looked at the names with unseeing eyes. "I don't feel much like a bride."

"But why?"

A tear traced a wet trail down Julie's pale cheek. "Daniel's busy right now. It seems I hardly see him."

Sherry rolled her chair close to Julie's desk and handed her friend a tissue. "Believe me," Sherry said sympathetically, "I know the feeling of abandonment well. That's how all my problems with Andy started. He worked so many long hours that we didn't have time to be a couple anymore. He was so involved with his job that eventually we drifted apart. It got to be that he was home so little of the time that I'd been gone a week before he even knew I was missing."

Julie tried to laugh but her voice came out sounding like a sick toad. Just then their employer came out of his office. He started to say something before noticing Julie blowing her nose. He paused, glanced from Sherry to Julie and quickly retreated into his office again. The two women looked at each other and broke into helpless giggles.

Ten minutes later, Mr. Barrett returned. "I was wondering..." he said and nervously cleared his throat. "Would you two like to take an extra half hour for lunch today? It's been a hectic week."

Julie and Sherry exchanged surprised glances. "We'd love it. Right, Julie?"

"Right," Julie concurred, doing her best to hide a second giggle. Poor Mr. Barrett, he didn't know what to think.

The long lunch with Sherry proved to be just the tonic Julie needed to raise her sagging spirits.

"You know," Sherry said between bites of her chicken and cashew salad, "if I had it to do all over I'd make it so Andy never wanted to leave the house again."

Julie stirred her clam chowder without much interest. Her appetite had been nonexistent lately and with little wonder. "How do you mean?"

"Think about it." Sherry leaned against the table, her eyes sparkling mischievously. "We're both reasonably attractive women. There are ways for a wife to keep a husband home nights." Demurely she lowered her thick lashes. "Subtle ways, of course."

"Of course," Julie repeated, her thoughts spinning. Sherry didn't know the details of her problems with Daniel, but her co-worker was so amazingly astute that Julie wondered if Sherry had somehow discovered her secret.

As the day progressed, Julie gave more thought to Daniel's actions. In the beginning he'd been bitter, but as the weeks progressed, time had healed that aggressive hostility. He'd told her after taking down their engagement photo that he wouldn't hurt her again. And he hadn't. If anything, he was all the more gentle with her. Only the other night, she'd found him holding their photo and studying their young, happy faces. Julie had held her breath, worrying about his reaction. She feared he would look at their picture and remember the pain and embarrassment she had caused him. Instead his gaze had held an odd tenderness. He hadn't known she'd seen him and she'd been puzzled when he retreated into his den. It made sense that if he'd forgiven her, if he loved her and wanted her, that he'd come to her. Julie was beginning to hate that guest bedroom. She didn't belong there; she was his wife, and she longed to be so in every way.

In the weeks since their wedding, Daniel had only touched and kissed her a few times and yet she'd seen the desire in his eyes. He wanted her. He spent the evenings avoiding her for fear of what would happen otherwise. His male pride and ego were punishing them both.

A secret smile touched Julie's eyes as she recalled the pearly-white satin nightgown she'd recently admired in a department store window. Perhaps she could do as Sherry suggested and lure her husband to her bed without injuring either of their sensitive egos. The more she contemplated such an action, the more confident she became.

After work that evening Julie and Daniel drove silently to the hospital. Mrs. Van Deen was sitting up in bed and smiled warmly, holding out her hand to Julie as they came into the room.

"My dears," she murmured with a happy light glinting from her tired eyes, "it's so good to see you."

"Mother." Daniel kissed her wrinkled cheek and held Julie close to his side with a hand at her neck.

"Julie, you're looking especially pretty. That color agrees with you."

Daniel looked at his wife as if seeing her for the first time that day. His eyes softened measurably as he noted the way the soft pink dress molded gracefully to her. A smile touched his eyes. "She certainly does," he said as his hand slipped around her waist.

"How are you feeling?" Julie centered her attention on Daniel's mother, thinking how good it felt when Daniel played the role of the loving husband. Soon he wouldn't be pretending, she vowed.

"Better," Clara said with a sigh. "The doctor said he'd never seen a woman make a swifter recovery. But I told him I have something to live for now. My son has the wife he's always wanted and I shall soon have the grandchildren I've dreamed about holding."

Daniel's fingers bit unmercifully into Julie's middle and she had to suck in her breath to keep from crying out. Her hand moved over his and it was an effective way of letting him know he was hurting her. Immediately, his grip slackened.

"My grandchild will have the bluest eyes," Mrs. Van Deen continued, oblivious to the tension in the room. "My husband's eyes were blue. So blue I swear they were deeper than any sea. I wish you'd known him, Julie," she continued, lost in a world of happy memories. "He would have loved you just as I do. He was a fine man."

"I'm sure he was," Julie replied thoughtfully.

"A lot like Daniel."

Julie glanced up at her husband; her eyes were captured by the warmth of his look. Daniel's mother continued speaking, reminiscing about her life with August Van Deen.

When Julie and Daniel returned to the condominium that evening Julie released a long sigh.

"What was that about?" Daniel asked gruffly.

"What?"

"That moan. Do you want me to apologize because my mother likes to remember the happy years she spent with my father?"

Julie stared back at him in shocked disbelief. She'd thought they'd made more progress than to have Daniel accuse her of something like that. "Of course not," she murmured, unable to disguise the hurt.

"Then why the sigh?" He remained defensive.

"I . . . I was thinking how much I wanted our lives to be as rich and rewarding."

"I'm sorry, Julie, I didn't mean to snap at you." Daniel's rich dark eyes softened before he turned and delivered his briefcase into his den.

"I understand," she whispered in return. It was nearly seven and they hadn't eaten dinner. They were both hungry and tired.

While the noodles were cooking, Julie changed clothes, donning tight navy-blue cords and a thin sweater that outlined the ripe fullness of her breasts. For good measure she refreshed her makeup and dabbed on Daniel's favorite perfume, then returned to finish preparing dinner.

Daniel looked surprised as he joined her in the kitchen. He studied her for a tense moment as if noting something was different.

"I didn't want to spill anything on my dress," she told him, hiding a smile.

He answered her with a short nod, but he couldn't seem to keep his eyes off her as she deftly moved around the tiny kitchen.

He didn't talk much while they ate, but that wasn't unusual. Perhaps Julie was reading too much into his actions. After so many years of living alone he could simply prefer to keep his thoughts to himself.

With seduction plots brewing in her head, every bite of her dinner seemed to stick in her throat and after a few minutes she stood and scraped half her dinner down the garbage disposal. Absently she placed her plate in the dishwasher.

"I thought I was doing dishes."

"There are only a few things."

"Hey, we made a deal. When you cook, I wash the dishes," he said. "Now scoot."

Having been ousted from the kitchen, Julie sat watching the television, but her mind was not on the situation comedy.

Daniel worked in the kitchen, but several times Julie felt his eyes rest on her. A couple of times she glanced up and smiled sweetly at him.

"A penny for your thoughts," he said, bringing her a cup of fresh coffee.

Julie swallowed a laughing gasp. "You wouldn't want to know," she teased. "You'd run in the opposite direction."

"That sounds interesting."

"I promise you it is."

Daniel surprised her by sitting in the wing-backed chair beside her. "Julie." He took the remote control and muted the television. "Can we talk a minute?"

"Sure." Expectantly, she turned toward him.

"I haven't been the best of company lately." He hesitated.

"There's no need to apologize," she told him. "I understand."

"How do you mean?"

"You must be exhausted. Heaven only knows when you sleep. You've been working yourself half to death this last month." Crossing her legs, Julie leaned back against the velvet cushion. "And then this evening your mother started talking about grandchildren and neither one of us has the courage to tell her we aren't sharing a bed." Nervously she glanced down at the steaming coffee. It was on the tip of her tongue to admit how much she wanted that to change, how much she longed to be his wife in the full sense of the word and give life to his children.

"Julie, listen." His voice was filled with a wealth of emotion.

The phone rang, directing their attention to the kitchen.

"I'll get it," Julie volunteered. Whoever it was, she'd get rid of him in a hurry. For the first time Julie felt like they were making giant strides in their marriage. Their conversation was far more important than someone who wanted to sell them siding for a house or steam clean their carpet. "Hello," she said into the receiver.

A pregnant pause followed.

"Hello," Julie repeated.

"Who's this?" the husky female voice returned.

"Julie Van Deen," she answered.

"So it's true," came the hushed words, coated with shocked pain.

"And you're . . . ?" Julie squared her shoulders, already knowing it had to be the woman Jim Patterson had mentioned on the tennis courts that day. A hundred times since, Julie had bitten back questions about the other woman. But something deep inside had held her back.

"Kali Morgan," the woman answered.

An icy chill raced up Julie's spine. "Would you like to talk to Daniel?"

Kali paused. "No. Just...just give him my best...to you both."

"Thank you," Julie murmured. Hurt and confused, she replaced the phone.

"Who was it?" Daniel was looking at her expectantly.

Twisting around, Julie clasped her hands together behind her back. "An old friend of yours." Her voice was incredibly weak.

"Who?" Daniel repeated.

"Someone who obviously didn't know you had a wife."

"Kali." The word was a statement, not a question.

All this time Julie had assumed that Daniel really wanted her as his wife. Now that she'd heard the shocked pain of the other woman's voice, Julie's confidence crumbled. "You didn't tell her, did you?"

Daniel stood, but the width of the living room remained between them. "Julie." He sounded unsure, worried. "What did Kali say?"

Her eyes searched his face, silently studying him. The man who stared back had become a stranger. Her heart throbbed painfully and she pressed her palm over it, not understanding how any pain could be so intense. Daniel seemed to think that he needn't tell Kali that he had married. Maybe he believed that given time, Julie would leave him and he could go back to his old life. As callous as it sounded, perhaps he was holding on to his options so that if his mother didn't survive this ordeal he could quickly annul their marriage. Maybe he was looking for ways to hurt her as she'd hurt him. If so, he'd succeeded. She'd been so stupid. So naive.

Slowly Daniel took a step toward her. "Julie, don't look at me like that."

Paralysis gripped her throat as she moved down the hall to her room. The bag containing her lovely new nightgown rested on the top of her bed. She stared at it in disbelief. Only minutes before she'd plotted to seduce her husband.

Daniel followed her down the hall. "Julie, be reasonable. Surely you didn't think I've lived the last few years like a priest."

Everything went incredibly still as hot tears filled her eyes, scalding her cheeks as they crashed over the wall of her lashes. "For three years my heart grieved for you until I couldn't take it anymore...and I came back because...because facing your bitterness was easier than trying to forget you."

"Julie." His voice took on a soft, pleading quality. He paused as if desperately searching for the right words.

"Kali and I have been dating for several months," he assured her. "But Kali's in the past. I haven't touched her since the day I saw you in the elevator."

"Touched her," Julie repeated shakily. "Is that supposed to reassure me?" she cried. "You haven't touched me either!" Her stomach heaved convulsively and she rushed into the bathroom.

Daniel followed her. Julie stood in front of the sink and pressed a cool rag over her face, attempting to ignore him.

"What did you expect me to do the rest of my life?" he shouted. "You walked out on me!"

Julie turned and raked her eyes over him with open disdain. "You didn't tell her we were married!" She hiccuped on a sob, convinced Daniel hadn't a hint why she was so upset. "And...and all these years I've loved you until coming back was better than facing life without you."

"Don't tell me that there hasn't been anyone in—"

"Yes," she shouted. "I seldom dated. You were the only man I ever loved. The only man I could ever love." She wept into the wash cloth.

"Julie," he pleaded softly, standing behind her, a gentle hand on each shoulder.

"Don't touch me," she shouted and shrugged her upper torso to break his light hold. "Your tastes have changed, haven't they, Daniel? You must find me incredibly stupid to have cherished the belief you still care.'' She couldn't finish and abruptly turned from him.

Roughly he pulled her into his arms. ''You're going to listen to me, Julie. Perhaps for the first time since we met one another we're going to have an honest discussion.''

Julie was in no mood to be reasonable. ''No,'' she cried, rushing back to her room. Grabbing the package from her bed, she shoved it in his arms. ''Here. Once I'm gone you might find this useful for one of your other women.'' With that she slammed the door, and collapsed into tears.

Sherry was at her desk when Julie entered the office the following morning.

''Morning,'' Julie greeted the other woman, doing her best to disguise her unhappiness. She knew she looked terrible. Cosmetics had been unable to camouflage the effects of the sleepless night. For the first time since their marriage, Daniel left for work without Julie. When she'd stirred with the alarm, the condominium had been as silent as a tomb and just about as welcoming.

''Morning,'' Sherry replied without looking up.

Although she was tied up with her own problems, it was obvious Sherry had been crying again. It took all her restraint not to join her friend and burst into tears. ''What happened now?'' Julie pried gently.

Wiping the moisture aside with the back of her hand, Sherry sat up and sniffled. ''After our talk yesterday, I got to thinking about how much I miss Andy...so I saw him last night.''

"Was he with another woman again?" That would explain Sherry's tears.

"No, this time he was with me. I . . . I told him I wasn't positive I wanted the divorce and that I thought we should talk things over more thoroughly before we take such a serious step."

"I think that's wise." Julie recognized how difficult it had been for Sherry to contact her husband and suggest that they meet. She and Daniel weren't the only ones with an overabundance of pride.

"We sat and talked for ages and, well, Andy ended up spending the night." She cast her gaze to the desktop. Her fingers nervously toyed with a tissue.

"Well it seems that not all lines of communication are down," Julie murmured, thinking how much she'd wanted to 'communicate' with her own husband.

"I . . . I thought so too. But this morning when I woke up, Andy was gone. No note. Nothing. He regrets everything; I know he does. Now I feel cheap and used and . . ." She paused and blew into the tissue.

"Sherry." While battling her own unhappiness, Julie moved behind the other girl and gently patted her back. Only the day before they'd been like teenagers, sharing girlish secrets. So much for the best-laid plans. Like a pair of idealistic fools, they had hoped everything would be perfect because they were in love with their husbands. "I'm sure there's a perfectly logical explanation why Andy left." Julie tried to sound optimistic, but knew she'd failed.

"I feel like a one-night stand."

"You are married." So was she, for that matter, and it didn't seem to help how she felt.

"Yes, but not for very much longer."

"Things have a way of working out for the best."
Julie tried to sound confident, but she didn't know
whom she was speaking to: Sherry or herself. "If you
love Andy then I wouldn't worry."

Sherry shook her head, doing her best to smile.
"How did everything go for you?"

"Fine," she lied and, at Sherry's narrowed look,
amended, "Terrible." Sniffling, she reached for a tissue.

The office door opened and Julie and Sherry immediately lowered their heads, pretending to be ab-
sorbed in their work. Mr. Barrett passed through the
room with little more than the usual morning greeting.

"He must think we've gone off the deep end,"
Sherry whispered once he was safely inside his office.

"Maybe we have."

"Maybe," Sherry agreed.

They worked companionably, taking turns answering the demands of the telephone. When she had a free
moment, Sherry lifted her purse to the desk and took
out her makeup case. "Count your blessings, Julie.
You're much too levelheaded to do some of the dumb
things I've done with this marriage. Can you imagine
anyone walking out and leaving a man as good as
Andy?"

Julie had to struggle not to confess that she had
done exactly that. "Maybe you should contact Andy
yourself," Julie suggested in a low voice that bordered on tremulous.

"I couldn't . . . not after what happened."

"I'm sure he'd be willing to talk, especially after last night," Julie insisted.

"I wish that was true," Sherry stated miserably. "But somehow, I doubt it."

Daniel was already in his den when Julie returned home that evening. Clara had let it slip that her son had been by earlier to visit. Her astute mother-in-law studied the dark shadows under Julie's eyes, but didn't comment. Julie was grateful. Her composure was paper thin as it was. Answering questions would have been her undoing.

Hanging up her jacket in the hall closet, Julie headed for the kitchen. A package of veal cutlets rested on the countertop and, releasing a sigh, Julie reached for the frying pan.

"I thought it was my turn to cook," Daniel said heavily from behind her.

"All right," she murmured without turning. "But I'm not very hungry. If you don't mind, I think I'll lie down for a while."

He was so long answering her that Julie feared another confrontation.

"Okay," he said at last. "I'll call you when dinner's ready."

"Fine." They were treating each other like polite strangers. Worse. They seemed afraid to even look at each other.

Flipping the light switch, Julie moved into the room and sat dejectedly on the side of the mattress. A month into her marriage and she was little more than an unwelcome guest in Daniel's life. The pillow comforted her head as she leaned back and closed her eyes.

It seemed only minutes later when Daniel knocked softly against the open door. "Dinner's ready."

Momentarily Julie toyed with the idea of telling him she wasn't feeling well. But Daniel would easily see through that excuse. No, it was better to face him. Things couldn't possibly get much worse.

The table was already set when Julie pulled out the chair and sat. Daniel joined her.

"Your mother looked better tonight."

Daniel deposited a spoonful of wild rice on his plate before he answered. "She asked about you. I didn't know if you'd be stopping in to see her or not."

"I did," she told him inanely.

"So I surmised."

Five minutes passed and neither spoke. Julie looked out the window and noted the thick gray clouds rolling in. Daniel's gaze followed hers. "It looks like rain."

Julie nodded. Since they had nothing in common—no shared interests—there was little to discuss beyond his mother and the weather.

Another awkward silence filled the kitchen until Julie stood and started to load the dishwasher.

"I'll do that," Daniel volunteered.

"It's my turn."

"You're beat."

"No more than you," she countered, stubbornly filling the sink with hot tap water.

The dishes took all of ten minutes. The hum of the dishwasher followed her into the hallway. The thought of spending another night in front of the television was intolerable. But going out was equally unsavory. Daniel had disappeared inside his den and Julie doubted that she'd be seeing him again that evening, which was just as well.

Deciding to read, she returned to her room. It wasn't until she turned that a glimmer of satin caught her attention. Setting the book aside, she discovered that the lovely, alluring gown she'd shoved at Daniel was hanging in her closet. Lovingly her fingers touched the silky smoothness. Tears jammed her throat. She'd so wanted things to be different. A soft sob escaped and she bit into the corner of her mouth.

"Julie." Daniel spoke from outside her room. "Are you all right?"

Angrily she turned on him. "I'm just wonderful. Just leave me alone." With a sweep of her arm, she closed her door, effectively cutting him off.

For a stunned moment nothing happened. Then her door was knocked open with such force that it was a wonder it wasn't ripped from the wall.

Julie gasped as Daniel marched into her room and lifted her from the floor and hauled her in his arms.

"Put me down," she cried, kicking her legs uselessly, but her efforts only caused him to tighten his grip.

"You're my wife, Julie Van Deen. And I'm tired of playing a game in which I am the loser." With that he marched down the hallway to his bedroom and slammed the door closed with his foot.

Chapter Eight

Furiously Julie wiped the tears from her face. "You didn't even tell Kali you were married," she shouted.

"I couldn't," he shouted right back. "She was in England on a business trip."

Julie's anger died a swift and sudden death. She went completely still and stared into her husband's dark, angry eyes. "Gone?"

"I don't know what's going on in that twisted little mind of yours. I'm not even sure why it matters if Kali knows or not. For heaven's sake—we're married. What the hell has Kali got to do with us now?"

She offered him a trembling smile through her tears. "Nothing," she whispered, laughing softly. "Nothing at all."

"What's so amusing now?" he barked, clearly not understanding the swift change in her mood. He sank onto the side of his bed, his hold on her loosening as she rested in his lap.

"You wouldn't understand," she murmured linking her arms around his neck and kissing the corner of his mouth. "I thought you were planning... Never mind." Gently she covered his mouth with hers.

"Julie," he groaned, his hands folding her in his embrace.

"Are you really tired of playing games?" she asked, spreading a series of sweet kisses over his face. Her eager lips sought his temple and nose, slowly progressing downward toward his mouth, teasing him with short, playful kisses along the way.

"Yes," he moaned, gripping the back of her head and directing her lips to his. "Oh, Lord, yes."

A pervading warmth flowed through her. "Oh, Daniel, Daniel, what took you so long?"

Slowly his hands slid across her breasts as he began unfastening the tiny buttons of her blouse. All the while his mouth moved over hers in eager passion. Frustrated with the small pearl-shaped fastenings, he abandoned the effort and broke the kiss long enough to try to pull the blouse over her head.

Breathless and smiling softly, Julie stopped him. "You've waited a whole month for me. Another thirty seconds shouldn't matter."

As she freed her blouse, Daniel cupped the soft mounds of her breasts and buried his face in the fragile hollow of her throat. "I couldn't live another month like the last one," he told her, his gaze drinking in the velvet smoothness of her ivory skin. "I couldn't sleep knowing you were just down the hall from me. Every time I closed my eyes all I could see was you. The only thing that helped was working until I was ready to drop.''

"Oh, love, and I wanted you so much.'' Sliding her hands up and down his muscled shoulders, she felt the coiled tension ease out of him.

Hungrily he devoured her mouth. "You're my wife, Julie, the way you were always meant to be.''

"I know, love, I know.'' Her heart singing, Julie gave herself to the only man she had ever loved. She had accomplished everything she'd set out to do in Wichita and more. So much more.

"Wake up, sleepyhead,'' Daniel whispered lovingly in her ear. "It's morning.''

"Already,'' Julie groaned, running her hand over her husband's muscular ribs and resting her head in the crook of his arm. Her eyes refused to open.

"Are you happy?'' Daniel asked, kissing the crown of her head.

"Oh, yes.''

"Me, too.'' In long soothing movements, he stroked her bare arm. "I never stopped loving you, Julie. I tried, believe me I tried every way I could to forget you. For a time I convinced myself I hated you. But the day I saw you in the elevator, I knew I'd been fooling myself. One look and I realized I'd never love another woman the way I love you.''

Raising her head, Julie rolled onto her stomach and kissed him with infinite sweetness, slanting her mouth over his.

The hunger of his response surprised her. Quickly he altered their positions so that Julie was on her back looking up at him. His eyes burned into hers.

"Daniel," she protested, but not too strenuously, "we'll be late for work."

"Yes, we will," he agreed, "very late."

An hour later, while Julie dressed, Daniel fried their eggs, humming as he worked.

"My, you're in a good mood this morning," she teased, sliding her arms around his middle and pressing her face against the muscular back.

Daniel chuckled. "And with good reason." He twisted around and pulled her into his arms, kissing her soundly. "I love you."

Her eyes drank in the tenderness in his expression as she slowly nodded. "I know."

"I think it's time we took that diamond ring hanging around your neck and put it on your finger, where it belongs," he told her gently. He helped her remove the chain and slid the solitaire diamond onto her finger with a solemnness that told her how seriously he took his vows. "I wanted you the minute the minister pronounced us man and wife," he admitted sheepishly. "I had to get out of the condominium that day because I knew what would happen if I stayed."

"And I thought—"

"I know what you thought," he said, taking her back into his embrace. "It was exactly what I wanted you to believe. My ego had suffered enough for one day. I couldn't tolerate it if you knew how badly I wanted to make love to you then." His chin brushed the top of her head.

The workdays flew by and after a wonderful weekend together, Julie and Daniel spent a quiet Sunday with his mother at the hospital. Clara Van Deen's heart surgery was scheduled for the next Tuesday and both Julie and Daniel wanted to be with her as much as possible.

"Have you told Julie about her surprise yet?" Clara questioned Daniel as he wheeled his mother into the brilliant sunshine of the hospital courtyard. The day was glorious, birds chirped a contented chorus and the sky was as blue as Julie could ever remember seeing it.

"Surprise?" Julie's attention wandered from the beauty of the day. "What surprise?"

"Oh, dear." Mrs. Van Deen twisted in the chair and glanced over her shoulder at her son. "I didn't let the cat out of the bag, did I?"

Leaning forward, Daniel kissed his mother's pale cheek. "Only a little," he whispered reassuringly. "I was waiting until later."

"Later?" Julie spoke again. "What's happening later? Daniel, you know how much I hate secrets."

"This one you'll enjoy," her husband promised. His eyes held a special light that was meant for her alone. He laughed at her puzzled expression and slid a hand around her waist and kissed her lightly on the cheek. "I won't make you wait any longer than this afternoon," he whispered in her ear. The tender look in his eyes was enough to make her feel light-headed.

After an hour in the glorious sunshine, Clara Van Deen announced in a frail voice, "I think it's time for me to go back inside. I tire so easily."

Immediately, Daniel stood, gripped the wheelchair and prepared to wheel her inside. "We shouldn't have kept you out so long."

"Nonsense," Clara protested. "I've been wanting to feel the sun for days."

Julie followed them back into the hospital corridor and her mother-in-law's room. Within half an hour Clara was in bed and asleep, her tired features relaxed.

Standing on opposite sides of the hospital bed with the railing raised, Daniel whispered, "Are you ready for your surprise now?"

Julie nodded eagerly. For days she'd been aware he was planning something. The last two mornings they'd driven to work separately because he had late business appointments. Or so he claimed. Julie wasn't sure. He had a gleam in his eye and several times he looked as if he wanted to tell her something, but swallowed back whatever it was.

During the past few days, Julie had never known such blissful happiness. Daniel was more tender and loving then she'd ever dreamed. It astonished her how much he desired and loved her.

Their hands joined, they strolled out of the hospital to the parking lot. Daniel opened and closed her car door for her and stole a lingering kiss when no one was looking.

"Aren't you going to give me any hints?" Julie felt his gaze rest on her warmly.

"Not a one. You'll just have to be patient," he admonished her gently.

He smiled at her and Julie felt the magnetic pull of sensual excitement only he was able to generate within her. Julie couldn't imagine loving him any more than she did right this moment, this hour, this day.

Daniel took the freeway that led out of town and drove past the densely populated suburbs. Finally, he exited and turned down a long winding road that led into the countryside.

"For heaven's sake, Daniel, where are you taking me? Timbuktu?"

He chuckled. "Wait and see."

Again Julie was pulled into the magnetic aura of this man she loved. Everything was so perfect. So right.

When he pulled the car into a long driveway that led to a newly built two-story house, Julie was awe-struck.

"What do you think?" His eyes sought hers; one brow lifted inquisitively.

"What do I think?" she repeated, feeling the waves of shock dissipate. "You mean this . . . house . . . is my surprise?"

"We're signing the final papers for it Monday morning. There are several things that are awaiting your decision. The builder needs to know what color you want for the kitchen countertop, the design of the tile for the bathrooms. From what I understand there are several swatches of carpet for you to look at while we're here."

Julie nodded, not knowing what to say. She couldn't understand why Daniel wanted a place so far from the city. It would mean a long drive both ways in heavy traffic every day. Julie loved the city. Daniel knew that.

"Come inside and I'll give you the grand tour." He climbed out of the car, walked around to her side and gave her his hand. "You're going to love this place."

Julie wasn't convinced as his words echoed through her numb brain. Why would he pick out something as important as a house without consulting her? Shock waves trembled through her body as Daniel took out the key and opened the front door, pushing it aside so she could enter before him. At first she was overwhelmed by the magnificence of the home. A sunken living room contained a massive floor-to-ceiling brick fireplace. The crystal chandelier in the formal dining room looked like something out of a Hollywood movie. No expense had been spared to make this home an opulent showplace. But the kitchen was compact and the only real eating space was in the formal dining room. Nor did the house have a family room.

"What do you think?" Daniel asked eagerly.

"Nice." Julie couldn't think of anything else to say. It was a beautiful home, that she couldn't deny, but it wasn't something she would have chosen. In many ways it was exactly what she wouldn't want.

"The swimming pool is this way." He led her to the sliding glass doors off the kitchen and to a deck. A kidney-shaped pool was just outside. Although the cement structure was empty, Julie could picture aqua-blue water gently lapping against the tiled side.

"Nice," she repeated when he glanced expectantly toward her, seeking her reaction.

"If you think this is impressive, wait until you see the master bedroom." Daniel took her limp hand and pulled her through the hallway.

The room was so huge that Julie blinked twice. Fireplace, walk-in closets, sunken tub in the private bath. Everything anyone could ever want. But not Julie.

"What about the other bedrooms?" By some miracle she was able to force the question from her parched throat.

"Upstairs." His low voice was almost a caress.

Like a robot Julie followed him up the open stairway. Three large rooms led off a wide hallway. Another bedroom and a bath. The second room, without a closet, Julie assumed would become Daniel's den. The third room looked as if it was meant to be an art room with huge glass windows that overlooked the front of the house.

Although she made the appropriate comments, Julie felt as if someone had a strangle hold on her throat. Speaking became nearly impossible and she didn't know how much more of this she could take. Abruptly, she turned and walked down the stairs.

"Julie." Daniel followed her out the front door. "What's the matter?" His troubled gaze pierced her numbed senses.

Shaking her head, Julie tilted her chin to the sky, and fought for control of her raging emotions. That Daniel would look for and buy a house without consulting her struck her like arrows from the past. Memories returned to haunt her. She wasn't a naive teenager anymore. His mother had picked out their first home as a wedding present without consulting Julie. And now Daniel was doing it again. Anger, hurt and a myriad of emotions seemed to swarm around her like troublesome bees, stinging her pride and wounding her ego.

"You don't like it, do you?" A hint of challenge was evident in his voice.

"That's not it," she admitted flatly. She was angry with Daniel, and equally upset with herself. Most women would love a home like this. Unfortunately, she wasn't one of them.

"All right," Daniel breathed, his gaze scrutinizing her. "What don't you like? I'm sure whatever it is can be changed."

"Changed?" she flared back. "Can you change the location? I love Wichita. I want to live in the city. You've lived there all your life so what suddenly made the thought of the country so appealing?"

"Peace, solitude—"

She didn't allow him to finish. "What about the hour's commute in heavy traffic every morning and night?"

"I'll get used to it," he said, attempting to reason.

Her eyes flashed angrily at him. "Sure you will."

Crossing his arms over his muscular chest he seemed to be physically blocking out her words. "Is there anything else?"

Julie swallowed at the lump choking her throat. "Three years ago I didn't say anything when your mother bought a house without me so much as looking at it. I let everything build up inside until it exploded and I fled. I can't do that anymore. This is a beautiful home, but it's not a place for us. Someday I'd like to have children. This house isn't a family home. It's for a retired couple, or for a family with teenagers." She waved her hand accusingly at the two-story structure that seemed to be laughing back at her with all its magnificence.

Daniel frowned and the action drove deep grooves into his forehead.

"I . . . I appreciate what you're trying to do, but—"

"Be honest, Julie. You don't appreciate a thing about this house." A cynical smile twisted his mouth. He held open the car door for her and shut it once she was inside.

She waited until he was in the driver's seat. "Daniel." His name rushed out in a low breath as she exhaled. "I'm sorry I sound so ungrateful. But something as important as a home should be decided upon by both of us." She drew in a shaky breath. "I realize you were saving this as a surprise and I'm sorry if I ruined that."

Either he was caught up in his own disappointment and didn't hear her or he chose to ignore her. The tires squealed as he pulled out of the long driveway and onto the road.

On the drive home Julie sat miserably with her arms crossed. Moving into that house feeling the way she did would have destroyed her hard-won resolve. She'd come too far in three years to allow something like this to happen to her a second time.

The silence in the car was deafening. Daniel had wanted to surprise her. Maybe she hadn't expressed her feelings in the most subtle way, but surely he recalled what had happened with his mother.

Daniel looked pale under his tan, or maybe it was her imagination, Julie didn't know. When they arrived back at the condominium, he went directly into his den and made a series of phone calls while Julie struggled to understand what had motivated him. A dark cloud seemed to hang over their heads. Only that afternoon, Julie had doubted that anything could destroy their utopia. Now she realized how fleeting their happiness was.

Julie was cooking their evening meal when Daniel joined her. With her back to her husband, Julie made busywork at the stove, needlessly turning the few slices of beef every few seconds. "I wish you hadn't closed yourself off in the den," she began nervously. "I thought we were beyond that. I think it's important that we talk this out."

He didn't answer her.

"Daniel," she pleaded and turned to find him sitting at the table, reading the newspaper. "Are you giving me the silent treatment?"

He lowered the paper. "No."

"Then let's talk." Again she spoke to the front page of the paper. "If...if that house means so much to you then I'll adjust." Making a concession like this was the most difficult thing Julie had ever done. But her marriage was worth more than her pride.

Apparently engrossed in his paper, Daniel didn't speak for several long minutes. "You're right, it wasn't a good idea for me to have taken the bull by the horns."

"Then why are you so angry?" she pleaded.

With a slow deliberate motion he set the paper aside and wiped a hand over his face. "I don't know," he admitted honestly. "My mother claimed when you left that you were ungrateful for all we'd done for you. I'm beginning to understand what she meant. I bought that house for you, Julie, and for our lives together."

Julie could hardly believe what she'd heard. "What a horrible thing to drag up now. You're being completely unfair."

"Was it fair of you to walk out on me three years ago? Don't talk to me about fair."

The color washed out of her face as the shock of his words hit her.

Oblivious to her pain, Daniel raised the newspaper and continued reading.

A full minute passed before Julie could move. Numb with emotional turmoil, she turned off the stove and walked out of the kitchen.

Daniel claimed to have forgiven her, but he hadn't. Not in his heart. Tonight he'd wanted to hurt her because of his disappointment.

"Julie." His voice was filled with regret.

She heard his chair scrape against the floor before he followed her into the living room. "I didn't mean that."

"I doubt if that's true. I believe you meant every word." Julie swallowed tightly and by the sheer force of her will restrained the tears.

"Maybe I did at that," he said tightly.

The next thing Julie heard was the front door closing softly.

The following morning Julie left the condominium early, not waiting for Daniel. She was already at her desk when Sherry arrived for work.

"You're punctual as always," Sherry commented as she sat in her rollback chair and stuck her purse in the bottom desk drawer.

"I try to be," Julie said without looking up from her paperwork.

"I'm going to run down and grab a maple bar and coffee. Do you want me to pick up one for you?"

"Sure," Julie agreed rather than make an excuse as to why she wasn't hungry. She was counting out the change to hand Sherry when the office door opened.

Framed in the doorway was Daniel. A muscle worked convulsively in his lean jaw as he glared at her. Julie could see and feel his anger and the effort he made to control it.

Sherry glanced from one to the other and took in a deep breath. "If you'll excuse me, I'll run downstairs."

Silently, Julie's eyes thanked her friend. Understanding, Sherry winked and edged her way past Daniel.

"Don't do that to me again," he commanded in a low growl.

"I needed some time alone," she explained. "I thought you'd understand that.... You felt the same way yesterday."

"That was different," he snapped.

"If you can vanish until the small hours of the morning without an explanation then I have the right to leave for work unannounced." Angry now, Julie was astonished at how level her voice remained.

The phone rang and she swiveled around to answer it, presenting Daniel with a clear view of her back. Halfway through the conversation, she sensed he'd left. She couldn't see him, but the prickly sensation at the back of her neck eased and she felt the tense muscles of her shoulders relax.

Sherry returned by the time Julie had finished with the customer on the telephone. Her eyes were filled with questions, but Julie didn't feel up to making explanations.

"You have tomorrow off, don't you?" she asked instead.

Julie had nearly forgotten. "Yes. Daniel's mother is going in for heart surgery."

A lump lodged in Julie's throat. With so many pressures tugging at Daniel he didn't need a cold war between them. Tonight, she'd insist they put an end to this. They were both adults and should be able to put their grievances aside.

The day dragged by and the visit with her mother-in-law that evening went well. Although Julie stopped at the hospital immediately after work, she learned that Daniel had already been and gone and they had only missed each other by a matter of a few minutes. If his mother noticed that anything was different, she said nothing.

Julie stayed later than usual with Clara. They chatted together, and talked about flowers, which Clara loved. Then the nurse arrived and gave the older woman a shot to help her relax. Julie stayed until she was confident Clara was asleep and resting comfortably.

Her heart burdened, Julie walked to the parking lot and her car. This misunderstanding with Daniel about the house couldn't have happened at a worse time. The first test of love in their marriage and they had both failed. Utterly and completely.

Daniel wasn't home when she came through the front door and Julie felt as if she were carrying the weight of the world on her shoulders. Where could he be? Briefly she wondered if he'd gone to Kali. Julie felt her heart constrict with pain. He wouldn't. She couldn't love him as much as she did and believe he could do something like that.

She forced herself to cook dinner, but had no appetite and only picked at the cutlet and salad. After washing her few dishes, she turned on the television. Every five minutes her eyes drifted to the wall clock. Where was Daniel? His mother was having major heart surgery in the morning. This was the time they needed each other more than ever. Julie turned off the television and went to bed.

Shadows flickered like old-time movies against the dark bedroom wall as Julie lay staring at the ceiling. Her tension-filled body produced a curious ache as if every part of her being was affected by the events of the past two days.

The front door clicked softly and Julie sat upright, her ears picking up even the slightest noise. When the sound of the first footsteps could be heard, she released her breath, unaware she'd been holding it. A quick look at the clock confirmed that it was after midnight.

Daniel paused in the open doorway of their room. Their eyes dueled in the dark. His were filled with challenge as if he dared her to comment on how late it was or demand to know where he'd been. She wouldn't, not when there were so many other things to say.

He loosened his tie as his eyes continued to hold hers in the moonlight. Still he didn't speak, his eyes mocking her with every movement as he took off the suit coat and carelessly tossed it over the back of a chair. The air in the room contained the stillness that settles over the earth before an electrical storm. Tension seemed to arc between them.

Frantically her mind searched for the right words. All the hours that she'd lain awake she could have been rehearsing what to say. Now her mind was a blank, empty.

Of its own volition, her hand reached out to him. For one heart-stopping moment Julie thought he was going to reject her. She watched as he stiffened and closed his eyes as though he couldn't bear to look at her. The dark lashes flickered open and with a muted groan he crossed the room and reached for her as a dying man reaches for life.

"I'm sorry," she whispered, the words rushing from her in a breathy murmur. "Oh, Daniel, I'm so sorry. We need each other now more than ever. Let's forget the house." She wrapped her arms around his neck and hugged him as if she could never let him go again. Julie discovered that she wanted to laugh away their hurts and at the same time had trouble restraining the tears of release.

Roughly his hands brushed the hair from her face and lifted it to study the light in her eyes.

Julie was confident every emotion she was experiencing was there for him to read.

"Julie," he groaned in a husky voice. The harshness began to leave his expression as if he couldn't believe the love she was offering him. He buried his face in the slim column of her neck and inhaled deeply. "I need you."

Julie understood what he was saying. "Yes," she breathed and weaved her hands through his hair, holding him against her. "I love you," she murmured, and with a contented sigh she pulled his mouth to hers.

An hour later, her head nestled against the cushion of his chest, Julie lovingly ran her fingers over her husband's ribs. "We can't settle all our arguments this way."

Daniel chuckled, his breath caressing the hairs at the top of her head. Gently his hand ran down the length of her spine and back in a soothing motion. "I think it has its advantages." His voice was both tender and warm.

"I feel terrible about Sunday. Everything I said and did was wrong. You wanted to surprise me and—"

"No." His hold tightened momentarily. "You were right. Anything as important as a house should be a mutual decision. Later when I got over being angry, I realized how unreasonable I'd been."

"I might not have overreacted if that hadn't happened before. It was like living a nightmare all over again." She shrugged one ivory shoulder, unsure of dragging the past into this moment. "Do you really want to live in the country?"

The pause was long enough to cause her to raise her head.

"Not if you don't," he answered finally.

"My home is with you." She felt his smile against her hair and nestled closer to his warm body. Something was troubling Daniel, something more than his mother's ill health and pending surgery. Whatever it was had to do with their marriage. Julie didn't know what, but she had the feeling she would soon.

Chapter Nine

Daniel paced the waiting room as Julie sat in the vinyl-cushioned chair and attempted to read. Repeatedly, her concentration wandered from the magazine and she glanced at her wristwatch.

"What time is it?" Daniel inquired with a worried frown.

What he really wanted to know, Julie realized, was how much longer it would be. The doctor had assured them the surgical procedure would take at least five hours, and possibly longer.

"Anytime now," Julie answered and exhaled softly. They'd been in the waiting room most of the day. A nurse came at noon and suggested Julie and Daniel have lunch. But Julie couldn't have forced down anything and apparently Daniel felt the same way.

Her husband took the seat beside her and reached for her hand. "Have I told you how much I love you?" His eyes filled with tenderness.

Before Julie could answer, the doctor, clad in a green surgical gown, walked into the room. His brow was moist and he looked as exhausted as she felt. Automatically, both Julie and Daniel stood. Daniel held onto her trembling hand with such force that her diamond cut into her fingers.

"Your mother did amazingly well," the doctor began without preamble. "Her chances appear to be excellent."

A pent-up breath escaped Julie's lungs and she smiled brightly at her husband, feeling as if the weight of the world had been lifted from her back.

"Can we see her?" Daniel inquired, his own relief evident in his voice.

Julie knew her husband well enough to know that he needed visual assurance of his mother's condition.

"Yes, but only for a few minutes. You both can go in. She'll be in intensive care for a few days, then if everything goes well she'll be placed on the surgical floor."

"How long will it be before she can come home?"

The doctor shook his head lightly. "It would be hard to say. As soon as two weeks, or as long as a month."

Julie had appreciated from the beginning the quiet support the doctors and staff had given regarding her mother-in-law's condition.

"Thank you, doctor." Julie gave him one of her brightest smiles. "Thank you very much."

With their hands linked, Julie and Daniel were led into the intensive care area. When Julie saw Daniel's mother her heart lurched. The tubes and bottles surrounding her mother-in-law gave the older woman a ghostly look. She was deathly pale. White hair against the white sheets... The figure blurred and for a moment Julie thought she was going to faint.

"Are you okay?" Daniel's voice was filled with concern as he placed a hand around her waist to hold her upright.

"I'm fine," she assured him, but was glad for the supporting arm.

Clara Van Deen's eyes fluttered open and she attempted to speak, but the words were slurred and unintelligible. She tried to lift one hand, but it was taped to a board to hold the IV in place.

Lovingly Daniel laid his hand over his mother's.

"I'm afraid I'm going to have to ask you to leave." The efficient looking woman in the spotless white uniform requested softly a couple of minutes later. "You're welcome to come back tomorrow, but for now Mrs. Van Deen needs to rest."

Julie thanked the nurse with a smile and watched an expression of tenderness move across her husband's face.

"We'll be back, Mother," he whispered softly.

The air outside the hospital felt fresh and clean. Julie paused to inhale several deep breaths. Although they had done nothing to require physical exertion Julie was exhausted. With her head resting against the back of the seat, she closed her eyes as Daniel drove the short distance to the condominium.

"Julie." A warm, caressing voice spoke softly in her ear. "Wake up. We're home."

Her eyes fluttered open and she did her best to suppress a yawn. "My goodness, I don't know why I should be so tired."

"We didn't get much sleep last night," he reminded her with a roguish grin. "And the way I feel right now we may not tonight either." He helped her out of the car and held her close to his side until they reached their door.

Daniel led her directly into the bedroom and pulled back the covers. "I want you to take a nice long nap and when you're rested Mother has ordered us to have a night on the town."

Julie opened and closed her eyes, already feeling the pull of slumber. Maybe today had been harder on her than she realized. "A night on the town?"

"I'm not teasing. Mother and I had a long talk yesterday and she feels that after we spent today at the hospital we deserve to go out."

Julie was about to protest.

"No arguing," Daniel said sternly, "Mother insisted."

The bed felt warm and welcoming. Daniel tucked her in and kissed her lightly across her brow.

"Aren't you going to rest?" Julie wanted to know.

"Honey, if I crawl in that bed with you it won't be to sleep." The sound of his chuckle was caressing and deep. He brushed the hair from her temple. "Actually I've got some papers to go over. That should take an hour or two. Just enough time for you to catch up on some sleep."

Julie relaxed against the fluffy pillow and pulled the blanket over her shoulder. Her mind drifted easily into happy, serene thoughts as she closed her eyes and sleep commanded the deepest recesses of her mind.

The next thing Julie knew, Daniel was beside her, holding her close, his breath fanning her cheek.

"Is it time to get ready for dinner?" she muttered, reveling in the delicious warmth of her bed and keeping her eyes closed.

"I think breakfast is more in order."

"Breakfast?" Her lashes flew up. "I couldn't have slept through the night. Could I?" She looked around, confused.

"I paraded a marching band through here late yesterday afternoon and you wouldn't budge."

Wiping the sleep from her face, Julie sat up and leaned against the oak headboard. "I can't believe I slept like that. I was dead to the world for fifteen hours or more."

"I imagine you're starved."

Strangely she wasn't. Even her usual morning cup of coffee didn't appeal to her. Once she ate breakfast, however, she realized how famished she actually had been.

"I'm sorry I ruined your night."

Daniel looked up from his plate and smiled tenderly. He reached out and traced the delicate line of her jaw. "You didn't ruin anything," he whispered. "Do you know how incredibly beautiful you are in your sleep? I could have watched you for hours. In fact I did."

Somewhat embarrassed, Julie lowered her thick lashes and shook her head. A finger under her chin raised it to meet his eyes.

"I lay awake last night, my heart full of love, and I realized I'm the luckiest man in the world."

"Yesterday was a day to think that. Your mother survived the surgery, and we've been given a second chance to build a solid marriage."

"Yes, we have," Daniel whispered, his mouth seeking hers.

"What did you and Daniel decide on this house business?" Sherry asked over lunch later that week.

Julie shrugged, and set aside her turkey sandwich. "It's on hold. We've more or less decided to wait until we had a reason to move."

Sherry averted her gaze. "Do you want to start a family right away?"

"Yes." And no. Julie hadn't been naive enough to believe that once they were sharing a bed everything would be perfect. It wasn't. The incident with the house had proven that. Daniel loved her, but Julie was convinced he didn't completely trust her. It was almost as if he were waiting for her to pack her bags and walk out on him a second time. Julie realized that only time would persuade him otherwise. And Julie wanted a secure marriage before they had children.

After finishing lunch, the two women returned to work. The phone was ringing when they entered the office.

"I'll get it," Sherry volunteered, reaching for the telephone receiver.

Julie didn't pay much attention to the ensuing conversation until Sherry laughed and handed the phone to her. "It's for you. Personal."

"Daniel?"

"Nope, Jim Patterson."

Instantly Julie remembered Jim as Daniel's associate who had introduced himself the day of the tennis match. "Hello, Jim," she greeted cheerfully, somewhat surprised that he'd be contacting her.

"Julie. Sorry to call you at the office, but I didn't want Daniel to answer the phone and there was always that possibility if I rang your place."

"What can I do for you?"

"The Country Club has voted Daniel as The Man of The Year. We like to keep it a secret until the big night so don't let on that you know."

Julie's heart swelled with pride. "I won't breathe a word. Daniel will be so pleased."

"Each year we do a skit that tells the life story of the recipient of the award. You know, *This Is Your Life* type of thing. Of course we tend to ham it up a bit."

Julie giggled, her mind conjuring up the type of crazy stunts the men would pull.

"I was wondering if there was a time you and I could get together and go over some of the details of Daniel's life. I'd talk to his mother, but apparently she's in the hospital."

"I'd be happy to do that. When would you suggest?"

They agreed on a time and Julie was beaming with pride when she set the telephone receiver in its cradle.

"What was that all about?" Sherry inquired, not bothering to disguise her curiosity.

"Daniel's been named the Country Club's Man of the Year."

"That's wonderful!"

"I think so too," Julie agreed.

Daniel came into her office at quitting time. Usually Julie walked down the one flight of stairs to his suite and waited for him. But she was the last one to leave today, having made arrangements to stay a few minutes later to sign final escrow papers with a young couple. Both husband and wife worked full time and couldn't make it into the office any earlier than five. Julie was with the Daleys when Daniel walked through the door. She hadn't told him she would be later tonight, but not because she'd forgotten. Usually she was left waiting ten or fifteen minutes in his office and didn't think these few minutes would matter.

Julie smiled at her husband and gestured with her hand for him to take a seat. "I'll be done in a minute," she told him.

"I didn't realize it was so late." Mrs. Daley cast Julie an apologetic smile, glancing up from her wristwatch. "We've got to pick up the baby at the day care. You don't need me to sign anything more, do you?"

Quickly, Julie scanned the documents. "No, you're both free to go as soon as I've received the cashier's check."

"I've got that now," Mr. Daley announced.

Completing the transaction took only a few minutes longer. Mr. Daley enthusiastically shook Julie's hand and thanked her again for her help. This was the part of her job that she enjoyed the most. The house the Daleys were buying was their first and a dream they'd saved toward for three years.

The Daleys left the office and Julie quickly sorted through the remaining paperwork.

"Why couldn't Sherry have stayed?" Daniel asked stiffly.

"Because I volunteered," she answered on the tail end of a yawn. Placing her hand over her mouth, she lightly shook her head from side to side. "I don't know what's the matter with me lately. I've been so tired."

Daniel set his briefcase aside and claimed the chair recently vacated by the young husband. "I don't understand why you continue to work. There's no need. I make a decent living."

"I'd be bored if I didn't work." Julie immediately shelved the idea, surprised he'd even suggest it.

"You might have the time to learn how to cook."

"Are you complaining about my meals?" she joked, knowing he had every right to grumble. As long as she stuck to the basics, she was fine. But their menu was limited to only a handful of dishes and Daniel was obviously bored with the lack of variety.

"I'm not actually complaining," he began, treading carefully. "But I want you to give serious consideration to quitting your job. I don't like the idea of you having to work so hard."

"It's not hard," she protested. "And I enjoy it. Sherry and I make a great team."

"Whatever you want," he grumbled, but he wasn't pleased and Julie couldn't understand why.

A week after open-heart surgery and Clara Van Deen was sitting up in bed looking healthier than Julie could remember since returning to Wichita.

"I can't tell you how grateful I'll be to go home," she said, her voice rising slightly with enthusiasm. "Everyone's been wonderful here. I can't complain, but I do so miss my garden."

"And your garden misses you," Julie said with a wink to her husband.

"That's right, Mother." Looking grave, Daniel shook his head. "Weeds all the way up to my knees. I can hardly see the flowers in what was once the showplace of Willowbrook Street."

Clara Van Deen grimaced and shook her head. "I can't bear to think of what months of neglect have done to my precious yard."

Unable to continue the game any longer, Julie patted her mother-in-law's hand reassuringly. "Your garden looks lovely. Now don't you fret."

"Thanks to Julie," Daniel inserted. "She spent a good portion of the weekend on her hands and knees weeding."

"I should have been thinking of ways to torture a husband with a loose tongue," Julie admonished with a sigh. "It was supposed to be a surprise."

"My dear, Julie. You didn't really?"

"She has the blisters to prove it," Daniel inserted.

"Daniel! I didn't know your mouth was so big."

The hand across her back gently squeezed her shoulder. "All the better to kiss you with, my dear."

Julie tried unsuccessfully to hide a smile. "It's times like these that I wonder what kind of family I married into."

"One that loves you," Clara Van Deen replied with a warm smile. "Say, Julie, isn't today the day you were meeting with—"

"No," she interrupted hurriedly, warning her mother-in-law with her eyes not to say anything more. After Jim had contacted her about Daniel's award, Julie had shared the good news with his mother. Apparently the older woman had forgotten that the award was supposed to be a surprise.

Daniel made a show of glancing at his watch. "What's this about Julie meeting someone?"

"Nothing," Julie returned hastily.

"It's a surprise, son." The lined mouth twisted with self-derisive anger. "I nearly let the cat out of the bag the second time. Forgive an old woman, Julie."

"There's nothing to forgive."

"Will you two kindly let me know what is going on?"

"My lips are sealed," Julie taunted.

"Mine, too," Clara chimed and shared a conspiratorial wink with her daughter-in-law. "It's sometime this week, isn't it?"

Julie knew Clara was referring to her meeting with Jim. "Yes, over lunch. I'll let you know how everything goes."

"I will," Julie promised, squeezing Clara's hand.

Daniel's expression altered from amused to concerned on the way to the hospital parking lot. "You're not going to tell me, are you?"

"Nope."

"At least let me know whom you're meeting with."

"Never."

"I could torture it out of you," he whispered seductively.

"I'll look forward to that." She slid an arm around his waist and smiled up at him. He looked so handsome that she couldn't resist stealing a kiss.

"What was that for?"

"Because I love you."

A brief look passed over his features. One so fleeting that Julie was almost sure she'd imagined it. But she hadn't. Daniel doubted her. After everything that had transpired between them, her husband didn't believe she loved him. Julie was so utterly astonished that she didn't know what to say or how to react. Time, she told herself, he only needed time. As the years passed he'd learn.

On the ride home, Julie was introspective. They'd traveled this same route so many times over the past six weeks that sights along the way blended into one another.

"Daniel?" Julie sat upright.

"Humm?"

"Take a right here," she directed, pointing with her hand.

"Whatever for?"

"There's a house on the corner that's for sale." They must have passed the place a thousand times. Julie had noted the realtor's sign on each occasion and hadn't given the place a second thought. Now something about the house reached out to her.

Daniel made a sharp right-hand turn and eased to a stop at the tree-lined curb in front of the older, two-story Colonial home. The paint was peeling from the white exterior and several of the green shutters were hanging by a single hinge. "Julie," he groaned, "it doesn't even look like anyone lives there."

Julie glanced around her and noticed the other homes in the neighborhood. They were family oriented and well maintained. "All this place needs is a bit of tender, loving care."

"It's the neighborhood eyesore," Daniel said with more than a hint of impatience.

"I'd like to see the inside. Can we contact the realtor?" Already she was writing down the phone number.

"Julie, you can't be serious."

"But I am."

That same evening they met the realtor. "I'm afraid this place has been vacant for several months," James Derek, the realtor, told them.

"What did I tell you?" Daniel whispered near her ear. "This isn't what we're looking for—"

"No," Julie interrupted as she climbed out of the car, "but I like it. I like it very much."

"Julie," Daniel moaned as he joined her on the cracked sidewalk that led to the neglected house.

James Derek hesitated and Julie sensed that his sentiments were close to Daniel's. Undoubtedly, because of its run-down condition, this home would mean a much lower sales commission than the newer, more expensive homes they could afford.

"Can we go inside?" She directed her question to the realtor.

"Yes, of course."

The moment Julie walked through the door she knew. "Daniel," she breathed solemnly, her hand reaching for her husband, "this is it. This is the house."

"But, Julie, you haven't even looked around."

"I don't need to, I can feel it."

The entryway was small and led to an open stairway and a long mahogany banister that rounded at the top of the steps. To her right was a huge family living room and to her left a smaller room obviously meant to be a library or den. Dust covered everything and a musty smell permeated the house. The hardwood floors were dented and badly in need of buffeting.

"You'd probably want to have these old floors carpeted," the agent suggested.

Julie tossed him a disbelieving glare. Maybe oriental rugs, but it would be a shame to cover those solid wood floors.

The formal dining room had built-in china cabinets and a window seat. The kitchen was huge with a large eating area. The main level had two bedrooms and the upstairs had three more. The full basement was ideal for storage.

"It doesn't have a family room," Daniel commented after a silent tour. "That's something you've insisted on with the other house." His look wasn't encouraging and Julie realized he was grasping at straws.

"This house doesn't need one," Julie insisted. Desperately she hoped that Daniel could see the potential of the house. "It's perfect. Right down to the fenced backyard, patio and tree house."

"Perhaps you'd care to make a few comparisons with some other homes," the realtor interjected.

Determined, Julie shook her head. "I wouldn't." Her eyes met Daniel's. She realized their tastes were different. She even understood his doubts. This house would require weeks of expensive repairs, but the asking price was reasonable. Far below anything else they'd seen.

"In all fairness I feel you should be aware of several things."

James Derek's voice seemed to fade into the background as Julie sauntered from one room to the next. Her mind was whirling at breakneck speed as she viewed each room the way she would decorate it. Two bedrooms downstairs were ideal. After their family was old enough to move upstairs she could use that room as a sewing area. Next she wandered through the kitchen. The only problem she could foresee was having the washer and dryer in the basement. But the back porch was large enough to move the appliances out there. Of course, that would require some minor remodeling.

"Julie." Daniel found her and placed a hand on her shoulder. "I think we should go home and think this over before we make our final decision."

"What's there to decide?" For an instant she couldn't understand his reluctance. "If we don't put down earnest money now, someone else will."

"That's highly unlikely, Mrs. Van Deen," the realtor interrupted. "This place has been on the market for six months."

On the drive back to the realtor's office it was all Julie could do to keep her mouth shut. Before she and Daniel climbed into their own car, Daniel and James Derek scheduled another time for them to go and look at other houses.

With a numbed sense of disbelief, Julie closed her car door and stared straight ahead.

"Why'd you do that?" she demanded when Daniel climbed into the driver's side of their car a few minutes later.

"Do what?" He looked surprised at the anger in her voice.

"Set up another appointment."

"To look at houses—"

"But I've found the one I want," she declared. "Daniel, I love that house. We can look for another ten years and we wouldn't find anything more perfect. And best of all it's only a few blocks from your mother's. It's got a den for you and..."

"That house would be like living in a nightmare. The repair cost alone would be more than the value of the house. The roof's got to be replaced. There's dry rot in the basement."

"I don't care," Julie stated emphatically.

"I'm not going to fight with you about it. If we're going to buy a house then it's one we both agree on."

Julie had no argument. That house was everything Julie wanted. Hot tears brimmed in her eyes and blurred her vision. Something was definitely the matter with her lately. She couldn't believe she would cry over something as silly as a house.

The day Clara Van Deen came home from the hospital was the happiest Julie could remember. With Mrs. Batten's help Julie had the house spotless.

Although weak, the smile on her mother-in-law's face was reward enough for the long hours Julie had spent weeding and caring for her much-loved garden.

Mrs. Batten arranged huge floral bouquets around the living room and cooked a dinner of roast, potatoes and fresh strawberry shortcake, which had long been a family favorite.

Sitting with Clara on the patio, in the late afternoon sun, Julie lifted her face to the golden rays.

"Is everything all right with you, dear?"

The abrupt question surprised Julie. "Of course. What could possibly be wrong?"

Clara took a sip of tea from the delicate china cup. "I'm not sure, but you haven't been yourself the last couple of weeks. Has this house business got you down?"

"Not really." Julie straightened in the wrought-iron chair. The question struck a raw nerve. "Daniel and have more or less agreed to wait. There's no rush."

"But there was one house you liked?"

Julie knew the smile of reassurance she gave her mother-in-law spoke more of disappointment than any confidence. "We agreed to disagree." She changed the subject as quickly as possible. "Have you noticed how pink the camellias are this year?"

Clara didn't answer; her look was thoughtful. Daniel's look was almost identical when he unlocked the front door of the condo an hour later.

Julie felt uncomfortable under his gaze. "Is something bothering you?"

Daniel's mouth twisted wryly into a smile. "I thought we agreed not to take our disagreements to my mother."

Julie blanched, understanding immediately what had happened. Clara had spoken to Daniel about the house. "We did," she admitted stiffly.

"Mother had a talk with me before we left tonight."

"I know what it sounds like," Julie cut in, "but please believe me when I tell you that I didn't do anything more than mention it. I tried to change the subject."

A brooding silence followed and Julie watched as her husband's mouth thinned with impatience.

"If anything," she said, pausing to exhale, "I think I should have a talk with your mother. She's going to have to learn that although we love her dearly, she can't become involved in our lives to the point that she takes sides of an issue. Okay?"

"Definitely."

Julie walked across the room, her arms cradling her middle in an instinctively protective action. They were both walking on thin ice. Each desperately wished to maintain the fragile balance of their relationship. In some ways they seemed to be miraculously suited to each another and in other ways they were complete opposites. The house was a prime example. Daniel preferred the ultra-modern home. But Julie wanted something more traditional. She didn't know if they would ever be able to compromise.

Daniel cleared his throat and came to stand behind her. "I can see that this house issue could grow into a major problem."

Julie gave a determined shake of her head. "I won't let it. As far as I'm concerned all I want is to be your wife. It doesn't matter where we live."

His arms went around her and gathered her close within his loving circle. "I've been giving the house you wanted considerable thought," he whispered in a grave voice.

"And?" It was difficult to maintain her paper-thin poise.

"I think that we should be able to come up with a compromise."

"A compromise?"

"Yes." He drew back, his hands linked at the small of her back as he smiled at her upturned face. "I'll buy it if you agree to quit your job."

Chapter Ten

"Quit my job?" Julie repeated incredulously. "You have got to be joking." Her eyes studied the lines of strain about Daniel's mouth.

"That house is going to need extensive remodeling. Someone should be there to supervise the work."

Again her wide, troubled eyes searched his face. "It isn't remodeling the house needs, but repairs, most of which will have to be done before we move in." Breaking from his hold, Julie walked to the far side of the room. "I've seen it in you several times, but didn't bring it up hoping—"

"You're speaking in riddles," Daniel countered.

"The house isn't the real reason you want me to quit."

"I want you to be my wife."

"And I'm not now?" she responded in a stark voice. "I enjoy my job." Her hand made a sweeping gesture, slicing the air in front of her. "I've seen it in your eyes, Daniel. You think I'm going to walk out on you again. It's almost as if you're waiting for it to happen."

"You're being ridiculous."

"Am I?" she asked softly. "First it was the house you bought me that happened to be an hour out of town. It was like you wanted to close me off from the rest of the world."

Daniel stalked across the living room floor, and ran a hand along the back of his neck.

"And most recently you've suggested I quit working."

"I saw you with Jim Patterson last week," Daniel announced harshly.

"And you immediately jumped to conclusions."

"No." He turned around and Julie noted the heavy lines of strain around his eyes. She'd known something was wrong for days, but couldn't put her finger on it. He held her and loved her and gave no outward appearance that anything was troubling him. Only at odd moments when she caught him looking at her and witnessed the doubt and pain in his eyes did she guess.

"Will you tell me why you and Jim found it necessary to have lunch together?"

"I can't," she whispered miserably. "But I'm asking you to trust me. Surely you don't believe Jim and I are involved in any way?"

"I've tried. A hundred times I've told myself that you must love me. You wouldn't have come back or married me if you didn't."

"I do love you," she cried. "What makes you think I would even look at another man?" The hurt she was feeling must have been expressed in her eyes.

Daniel lowered his gaze and ran a hand over his weary eyes. "Sometimes I hate myself." The admission came with a bitter laugh.

"You don't trust me."

His returning look confirmed her worst suspicions. A sob rose to her throat, but she inhaled a deep breath and forced it down. "I love you so much I could never think about another man, nor could I leave you. What will it take to convince you of that?"

Daniel couldn't meet her eyes. "I don't know." He paced the carpet in front of her. "When I first saw you with Jim, I felt sick inside, then explosive. Even though I'd heard you joke with my mother about this meeting, I couldn't believe I'd see my wife and a good friend together. For two days I expected to wake up and find you gone."

"You actually believe that I'd run away with Jim Patterson?"

"Why not? You ran away from me before."

Julie closed her eyes feeling frustrated and furious. "I haven't even thought about anyone else since I moved to Wichita."

"But you had lunch with my friend."

"Yes." She couldn't deny it and wouldn't have, even if she could have lied.

"And you won't tell me why you met him?" He scowled.

"No. I'm asking you to trust me."

His dark eyes narrowed. "I'm trying. Lord knows I want to, but I don't know if I can," he whispered, his eyes revealing his torment.

"Julie, you don't look as if you slept at all last night," Sherry said when Julie walked into the office the following morning.

"I didn't."

"Why not?"

Julie had felt the weight of the world pressing down on her when they'd gone to bed after their discussion. Daniel stayed on his side of the mattress and although they were separated by only a few inches, he could well have been on the other side of the world for all the warmth and comfort they shared.

"It's a long story," Julie answered finally. She made busywork around her desk for a couple of minutes, then asked, "What would you think if I told you that Daniel wants me to quit my job?"

"Does he?" Sherry's baby-blue eyes rounded with concern.

"Let's make this a hypothetical question."

Julie wondered if, without knowing the background of her relationship with Daniel, Sherry would read the same meaning into her husband's strange behavior.

"Well, first off he wanted to move you into that house in the boondocks," Sherry said thoughtfully, rolling her chair the short distance between their two desks. "And now he wants you home all day. My guess is that he's insecure about something. But I can't imagine why. It's obvious to anyone how much you love him."

"I only wish Daniel recognized that."

"You're not going to quit working, are you? I suppose I'm being selfish," Sherry admitted sheepishly. "You've helped me so much through this ordeal with Andy. I can tell you things I wouldn't speak of to anyone else. I'd miss your friendship."

"No, I'm not going to do it." She refused to give in to his insecurities. Doing so could lead to an unhealthy pattern in their marriage that she wanted to avoid. "Enough about my problems. How's everything between you and Andy?"

"I get depressed so easily." Sherry lowered her gaze to her desk. "Who would ever have thought wooing my husband back could be so difficult?"

Julie smiled secretly to herself. She knew exactly what Sherry meant. She was shocked by how far she had to go to mend the hurts of the past three years.

The phone buzzed and Sherry looked up. Suddenly pale, she motioned for Julie to answer it as she rushed into the bathroom. Not for the first time in the past couple of weeks, Julie suspected her friend was pregnant.

Julie was off the phone by the time Sherry returned. "Are you going to tell me or are you going to make me ask?"

"How'd you know?" Sherry protested.

"Sherry, honestly. I can't believe you sometimes. I'd have to have my head buried in a hole not to have guessed. Does Andy know?"

Bright tears sparkled from her eyelashes. "No. If we do get back together, I want it to be because he loves and wants me. Not because of the baby."

"The divorce proceedings were halted, weren't they?"

Sherry nodded. "But only because Andy and I felt we needed time to think things out more thoroughly. We're not living together."

"You're not going to be able to hide it from him much longer," Julie advised softly.

Sherry propped her chin up with the palm of one hand and shrugged her shoulder. "I know. That's why I've given him three weeks to decide what he wants. If I'm going to lose him, then I'd prefer to face that now and be done with it."

"How does Andy feel about having an ultimatum?"

Sherry giggled and the tears glistened in her eyes. The contrast reminded Julie of a rainbow.

"Andy doesn't know."

"Oh, Sherry," Julie groaned.

A tear slid down her friend's cheek. "I realize this whole scheme sounds crazy, but I've thought everything out. I firmly believe I'm doing the right thing. I Andy found out about the baby and we reconcile then I'd never be sure. This way I'll have the confi dence I need that Andy really loves me and wants t make this marriage work."

The phone rang again and the two were quickly involved in the business of maintaining an escrow office.

Not until that night when Julie took pains to cook Daniel's favorite dinner did he notice something was different.

"Did I miss something?" he asked teasingly.

"Miss something?"

"It's not my birthday, is it? I've got it! You overdrew the checking account. Right?"

"Just because I cook stroganoff does it mean I'm up to something?" Julie inquired with feigned righteousness.

"In my short experience as a husband, my immediate reaction is...yes!"

"Well, you're wrong. I've taken all your complaints to heart and bought a cookbook. I can't have my husband fainting away from lack of the proper nourishment."

"Would you like me to demonstrate how weak I am?" he asked, slipping his hands over her breasts and pulling her against him.

"Daniel, not now."

"Why not?" he growled against her neck.

"Dinner will burn."

"That has never bothered you before."

"I thought you were hungry."

"I am. Come to bed and I'll show you how hungry am."

Julie switched off the stove and turned into her husband's arms, meeting the hungry urgency of his kiss with a willingness that surprised even Julie. She did love this man. Someday he'd realize how much.

Dusk had settled over the city before they stirred an hour later. Lovingly, Daniel's hand caressed her bare shoulder. "I'll be happy when you're pregnant," he whispered.

Involuntarily Julie stiffened. "Why?"

She could feel Daniel's frown. "I thought you wanted a family."

"I do." But she wanted the two of them secure in their marriage before they started a family.

"Then why the questions?"

"I want to know why you want a baby." A chill settled over the area of her heart. Her greatest fear was that Daniel would see a child as the means of binding her to him.

"For all the reasons a man usually wants to be a father." He tossed aside the blankets and sat on the edge of the mattress. "As I recall, we agreed that when you were pregnant, you'd quit your job."

Reaching for her robe at the foot of the bed, Julie buried her arms deep within the blue silk. She didn't know how any man and woman could make such beautiful love together and then argue. "I think you should know I've made an appointment with the doctor."

The silence grew and grew.

"So you think you might be pregnant."

"No, I want to make darn sure that doesn't happen."

As the days passed Julie had never been more miserable. Daniel treated her with icy politeness as if she were little more than a guest in her own home. If she'd thought the first days of their marriage were a test of her love it was nothing compared to the cold war that was being waged between them now.

Daniel threw himself into his work and Julie did her best to give the outward appearance that everything was fine. With Daniel gone so much of the time, Julie spent more and more of her evenings with her mother-in-law.

The two women worked at getting Clara's beloved yard into shape. Julie did her best to disguise her unhappiness, but she was convinced that her mother-in-law knew something wasn't right.

"I was surprised to see that old engagement picture of you and Daniel on the television," Clara remarked casually, working the border of the bed. Clara had recently visited the condominium for the first time since Julie and Daniel's marriage.

"We both look young, don't we?" Julie asked wistfully.

"It's difficult to remember you like that."

Julie had the impression her mother-in-law wasn't referring to looks. "We've all changed."

They continued working, each silently caught up in changes the years had produced.

"Something's bothering Daniel," Clara announced, studying her daughter-in-law closely.

"Oh?"

"I saw him briefly the other day and was shocked by his appearance."

"He's been working a lot of extra hours lately."

"Is it necessary?"

"I . . . I don't know." Avoiding her mother-in-law's gaze, Julie weeded another section of the flower bed.

"You look a bit peaked yourself," Clara Van Deen continued. "What's the matter with you two?"

Settling back on her heels, Julie sighed heavily. "Clara, Daniel and I agreed . . ."

"I know," she murmured. "Daniel said the same thing. But I can't help worrying about you both. You love each other and yet you're obviously miserable."

"I do love Daniel."

"And he loves you. I don't know that he's ever told you, but he knew where you were in California. All these years he's known and loved you. Whatever is bothering you two can't be worth all this torment. Believe me I know how stubborn my son can be. Just be patient with him."

"I'm trying," Julie whispered, struggling not to cry.

Back at the condominium an hour later, Julie soaked in a tub filled with hot water and perfumed bubble bath. She had no idea where Daniel was. Although it was Saturday, he'd left early that morning before she was awake.

Julie had hoped that a bubble bath would raise her spirits. Her head rested against the back of the porcelain bath. Forcing her eyes closed, she mused that without much effort she could easily fall asleep. She'd been so tired lately. It was ridiculous. It seemed she went to bed every night before Daniel and had trouble dragging herself up in the morning. That wasn't like her. Nor was the unbalanced diet she'd been developing lately. She was starving one moment and feeling like she'd overeaten the next. Her appointment with the doctor was in the first part of the week; she'd mention it to him. Her body had been doing funny things lately. It was probably a reaction to all the stress. Heaven knew she'd had enough of that to last a lifetime.

Abruptly, Julie sat up in the tub, causing hot water to slosh over the sides. In a flash she knew. She was pregnant. So much had been happening that she'd completely lost track of time. Biting into her trembling bottom lip, Julie leaned back and placed a hand on her flat stomach. Daniel would be pleased. This was exactly what he was hoping would happen. Despite her misgivings, Julie's heart swelled with joy. Just as quickly, tears flooded her eyes. She cried so easily these days and now she understood the reason why. All in one breath she was ecstatic with joy and unbelievably sad. Desperately she wanted this child, but she wanted the baby to come into a warm, secure marriage and not one torn by tension and mistrust. Sniffling, she wiped the moisture from her face.

Dripping water and bubbles over the bathroom floor, Julie climbed out of the tub and wrapped a towel around her body. An array of mixed emotions flew at her from all directions until she wanted to thrash out her arms to ward them off.

Sitting on top of their bed, she reached for the phone and dialed the number to Daniel's office where she suspected he'd be. The phone rang twice before

Julie abruptly cut the connection. What could she possibly say?

Sniffling anew, Julie dialed again and waited several long rings. "Sherry," she said, relieved that her friend was home. "Congratulate me, we're both pregnant." With that she burst into sobs.

Chapter Eleven

Here," Sherry said, handing Julie another tissue. "You're going to need this."

A dry-eyed Julie glanced at the Kleenex, then back to her friend. "I'm through crying. It was a shock, that's all." Within fifteen minutes after receiving the call, her co-worker and best friend had arrived at the condominium, flushed and excited.

"Discovering I was pregnant was a shock for me, too, if you recall. At first I was ecstatic, then I was flooded with doubts. Three days later I leveled out at 'great.'"

Julie's smile was wan. "A baby is exactly what Daniel wants."

"But for all the wrong reasons," Sherry claimed heatedly. "If Andy knew about me, I suspect he'd be thrilled; again for all the wrong reasons."

Julie nodded, feeling slightly ill. She hadn't eaten since breakfast, but the thought of food was enough to nauseate her.

"What did Daniel say?" Sherry sat across from Julie and laced her fingers.

"He doesn't know yet."

"You haven't told him?"

Julie laughed at the sound of incredulity in her friend's voice. "I learned that trick from you."

"What are you going to do?"

"I don't know yet. He has to be told, but I don't know when. He's . . . hardly around anymore."

"So he's pulling that trick again," Sherry huffed.

"He's working himself to death."

"Or he could be out having the time of his life as Andy did."

Julie doubted that. "I don't think so."

"Ha! That's what I thought about Andy. You aren't going to sit here and sulk. I won't let you."

"I'm not sulking."

"No, you're crying." She gave Julie another tissue. "Come on, I'm taking you out."

"Sherry, honestly, I appreciate your efforts, but the last thing in the world I want is to be seen in public. I look a mess."

"So, it'll take a bit of inventive application with your makeup."

"And twenty years."

Sherry giggled. "My friend, I'm going to let you in on one of life's important secrets."

"Oh?" Julie was dubious.

"When the going gets tough, then the tough go shopping."

"Sherry," Julie groaned. "I don't feel up to anything like—"

"Trust me, you'll feel a hundred percent better. Afterward I'll treat you to dinner."

"But Daniel..."

"Did he bother to tell you he wouldn't be home for dinner the last three nights?"

"No." She lowered her gaze to disguise the pain.

"Then it's time you quit moping around and do something positive for yourself."

Squaring her shoulders, Julie realized her friend was right. However Julie knew that Daniel probably wouldn't know she was gone. And worse, wouldn't care. If he was to return before she did, he would suspect she'd left him. It was almost as if he were driving her to that. Then her disappearance would only confirm what he believed would eventually happen anyway.

"All right," Julie agreed, "I'll go."

It took the better part of an hour to get ready, but Sherry was right, she felt better for it. Before they left the apartment, Julie penned Daniel a short note, telling him whom she was with. He may not care or want to know, but Julie felt better for having done it.

Sherry seemed intent on having a good time. First they frequented the mall stores, scouting out baby items and trying on maternity dresses until they laughed themselves sick.

Next they took in a movie and had an Italian dinner afterward. On the way home, Sherry insisted that they stop off at her house so Julie could see the baby blanket she was knitting.

"I think I'd better call Daniel," Julie said, sipping her cup of tea. The evening had slipped past so quickly. Already it was after eleven and although she had left the note, he might be worried. All right, she *hoped* he'd be worried.

"Don't," Sherry chastised. "He hasn't phoned you lately, has he?"

"No," Julie admitted reluctantly. She had barely seen him in the last week. They were like strangers who just happened to live together.

"I think I'll put on some music and let it soothe our souls."

"Good idea," Julie chimed.

The next thing Julie knew, she was lying on the sofa, wrapped in a thick comforter. Struggling to sit upright, she rubbed the sleep from her eyes so she could glance at her watch.

"I was wondering what time you'd wake up," Sherry called from the kitchen. "How do you want your eggs?"

"It's morning?" Julie was incredulous.

"Right, and almost ten. You were tired, my friend."

"But..."

"I turned on the radio last night and the next thing I knew you were sound asleep."

"Oh, good grief." Untwining the comforter from around her legs, she stood. "I'd better call Daniel."

"Go ahead. The phone's on the counter." She pointed to it with her spatula.

While Julie dialed, Sherry handed her a small glass of orange juice and two soda crackers. Julie smiled her appreciation. Her stomach was queasy and had been for several mornings. Only Julie had attributed the reason to nerves.

Ten rings later, she hesitantly replaced the receiver.

"No answer?" asked Sherry.

"No." Rubbing the palms of her hands together, Julie gave her co-worker a feeble smile. "Maybe he was in the shower."

"Maybe," Sherry echoed. "Try again in five minutes."

"At least he knows whom I'm with. If he was worried he would have called."

Sherry turned back to the stove. "He didn't know."

"I left a note."

"I stuck it in my pocket before we left your place. Heavens, I didn't know you were going to fall asleep on me and spend the night. I thought if Daniel worried a little it would be good for him."

"Oh, Sherry."

"It was a rotten thing to do. Are you mad?"

Julie shook her head, feeling utterly defeated. Sherry had no way of knowing that she had walked out on Daniel once and he was sure to believe she'd done it again.

"No," Julie mumbled. "He doesn't appear to be overly concerned at any rate. He's not even home." For that matter he could have returned late, as he had every night of the previous week, crawled into bed and not even noticed she was missing.

Fifteen minutes later, Julie used her key to open her front door. The condominium was dark, and absently Julie walked across the living room to open the drapes.

"Julie?"

Abruptly, she swiveled around to find Daniel sitting on the edge of the chair, leaning forward, his elbows braced against his knees. His dark eyes were wide and disbelieving.

"Hello, Daniel." He looked the picture of such utter dejection that she fought back the tears that clogged her throat. Julie didn't know how any two people who loved each other so much could come to this point.

Quickly the proud mask he wore slid into place and he stood, ramming his hands into the side pockets of his slacks. "I suppose you came back for your things."

"No." Somehow she managed to let the lone word escape. His clothes were badly wrinkled and his hair was rumpled as if he'd run his fingers through it several times. The dark stubble on his face was so unlike the neatly groomed man she'd lived with all these months that Julie looked away.

Apparently he didn't hear her. "Well go ahead and get them. Don't let me stop you."

"You want me to leave?" she asked, her voice little more than a breathless whisper.

"I won't stop you."

She dropped her gaze as the pain washed over her. "I see." Not knowing how to explain that she wasn't going, Julie took a step toward the hallway.

Daniel jerked his head up as she moved. His face was deathly pale, the fine lines about his mouth drawn and pinched.

"Julie." He murmured her name forcefully.

She turned back expectantly. Their eyes met and held. Neither seemed willing to break the contact. The tears filled her eyes and she wiped them aside with the back of her hand.

"I don't blame you for walking out on me," he spoke at last. "I drove you to it." He jerked his hand through his hair. "I let you out of my life the first time and blamed you for it. God help me, I can't do it again." He took a tentative step toward her. "Once you're gone, there won't be any more sunshine in my life. I lived for three long years in the dark and I won't go back to that. Julie—" his voice softened perceptibly "—don't leave me," he pleaded. "Let me make up for all the unhappiness I've caused you."

With a cry of joy, Julie reached out to him and they came together with all the desperation of young lovers separated by war. Daniel crushed her into his embrace and buried his face into her hair, taking in deep breaths as he struggled with emotion.

"It doesn't matter why you saw Jim or any other man. I was a fool to think everything would be solved by having you quit your job."

"Daniel, listen—"

"Moving into the country was just as ridiculous," he interrupted. "I love you, Julie, you're the most important person in my life. I can't let you go."

Cupping his ears, Julie lifted her head and spread tiny kisses over his face. "Would you kindly listen to me for one minute? I'm not leaving and never was. That was all a mix-up that we have to thank Sherry for. And as for my job, I plan to work for about another six months and then think about quitting."

"That sounds fair," he said and blinked. "Why six months?"

"Because by then the baby—"

"The baby?" Daniel repeated, stunned. His frown deepened as he searched her face. "Julie, are you telling me you're pregnant?"

Twenty-four hours ago, Julie would have been just as shocked had anyone mentioned her condition, but since then she had acknowledged and accepted the baby so readily that Julie had forgotten that Daniel didn't know.

"How? When?" He looked completely flustered.

Julie laughed and lovingly ran her hand along the side of his proud jaw. "You don't honestly need an answer to that, do you?"

"No," he agreed on a husky murmur. His eyes shone with pride and happiness. "All these weeks I'd hoped that you would be. I wanted a child to bind you to me. Now I realize how wrong that was. You've always been with me. Even while you lived in California, you were here in my heart."

Slipping her arms around her husband's neck, Julie smiled into the loving depth of his tender gaze. "We're already bound."

"By our love," he finished for her. When his mouth sought hers, Julie surrendered to her husband's deep hunger, secure in his love. "You needn't worry, Julie. I learned some valuable lessons about myself last night while I sat here alone. I was convinced my selfishness had driven you away a second time. What I didn't know was if I could bear to let you go." The doorbell chimed and Daniel glanced at it irritably. "I'll get rid of whoever it is," he promised, kissing the edge of her mouth with a fleeting contact that promised more.

"Hello," the man's voice came from the open door. "I'm looking for Julie Van Deen."

Julie cast an inquisitive glance at Daniel and shrugged. "That's me," she said, joining Daniel and looping an arm around his waist.

"Excuse me for intruding on you like this," he began as a pair of golden-brown eyes narrowed on her.

A salesman, Julie mused to herself, and one with the world's worst timing.

"I'm Andy Adams," he began haltingly, "Sherry's husband."

"Of course." Julie brightened immediately. "I've heard a lot about you."

"Yes." He cleared his throat and glanced at Daniel. "I'm sure you have. Sherry has mentioned you on several occasions."

"Come in. Can I get you a cup of coffee or something?"

"No, thanks. If you don't mind I'd like to ask you a few questions." He stepped into the condo, closing the door behind him.

"About Sherry?" Julie didn't want to get caught in the middle of her friend's marital difficulties, but knew that she probably already was.

"Yes. That is if you have no objections."

"I know that she's decided to stop seeing yo
and—"

"But why?" he demanded and paused to rumple hi
thick dark brown hair. "I apologize. I didn't mean t
shout."

He'd hardly raised his voice. "You didn't," she as
sured him. Andy and Sherry were as different as tw
people could be. Her flighty friend was married to thi
intense young man with the soft-spoken voice. Juli
would never have pictured Andy in a three-piec
suit.

"This whole thing is driving me crazy. I love m
wife. I loved her when we separated the first time. I
wasn't me who wanted that stupid divorce. Sherr
seemed to need space to find herself and I thought th
best thing I could do was give it to her, but I've a
ways loved her."

A soft smile touched Julie's eyes. "But then yo
decided to taste a little of that freedom yourself."

"It was all a game. I knew Sherry was going to b
there that night. By that time I was desperate an
thought a taste of her own medicine would help."

"It did," Julie returned, recalling her friend's r
action.

"A little too well," Andy admitted with a sel
derisive smile. "Maybe that was the mistake, I don
know. We were to the point of moving back in t
gether when—whamo—Sherry announces it's ov
and she doesn't want to see me again." He took a fe
brisk steps before pivoting and pacing back.

"I thought you were the one who—"

"No," he said forcefully. "It's true I thought this new relationship should progress slowly. I wanted Sherry to be sure of her feelings."

"I think she's very sure how she feels."

"But I thought—"

"Andy." Julie took in a deep breath. "I want you to think about something. When you and Sherry separated, she went off her birth control pills. Does that mean anything to you?"

The silence grew more intense with every passing second. "I'm going to be a father?" The words were issued in a disbelieving whisper.

"I'd say you've hit the nail right on the head."

"I'm going to be a father," he repeated as a contented smile lit up his eyes until they sparkled like rare jewels. "Then why in the sam hill did she tell me it was over? This doesn't make any sense."

"I think that's something you're going to have to ask Sherry."

"I will."

"Good." Julie couldn't help smiling.

"Thank you, thank you."

He took her hand and pumped it until Julie's fingers lost feeling, then reached for Daniel's hand, shaking it with the same enthusiasm.

"I've got to talk to Sherry."

"It'd be a solid bet to say she's anxious to see you."

"I can't thank you enough," he called as he opened the door and left, nearly tripping in his rush.

"I know exactly how he feels," Daniel said, taking his wife in his arms. "I feel like a fool who's been given a second chance at happiness. Believe me, this time I'm not going to blow it.''

"We're home," Julie said gently as she saw her mother-in-law rocking her three-month-old son a year later. She paused in the living room. Daniel had bought the house she'd loved and made extensive repairs. Most of the work they'd done together during Julie's pregnancy. "You know who you remind me of?" Julie asked, lifting the sleeping baby from Clara's arms.

"Probably Whistler's mother," the older woman answered with a soft chuckle. She had spent the evening with little Ted while Julie and Daniel attended a banquet at the Country Club.

"Was Jim surprised to be named Man of The Year?" Clara asked.

"Not anymore than I was last year," Daniel answered with a chuckle. "But then last year was a very good year."

"It was indeed," Clara murmured wistfully. "I was given a new lease on life."

"So was I." Daniel slipped an arm around his wife's trim waist and lovingly kissed the brow of his sleeping son.

Julie smiled down on her baby. "Was he good?"

"Not a peep. I must admit to being a bit frightened by him yet. He's so small. Theodore August Van Deen seems such a big name for such a tiny baby."

"He'll grow," Daniel said confidently. "And be joined by several more if his mother agrees."

"Oh, I'm in full agreement."

The baby let out a small cry.

"It isn't his feeding time, is it?" Clara looked up to Julie, the weathered brow knit with concern.

"Not yet," Julie assured her. "Don't worry, Grandma, babies sometimes cry for no reason."

"Teddy-boy, Grandma's joy." Clara took the baby from Julie and placed him over her shoulder. Gently, she patted his tiny back.

With infinite tenderness Daniel turned Julie into his arms, burying his face in the warm hollow of her throat. "I love you, Julie Van Deen." He raised his head and looked deeply into her soft blue eyes.

"And I you, my husband."

"The hurts and doubts are gone forever. I've buried my yesterdays."

"And look with happy excitement toward our tomorrows," she whispered softly and smiled.

COMING NEXT MONTH

SWEET MOUNTAIN MAGIC—Emilie Richards
They should never have fallen in love. But when astute, logical
Sarah MacDonald found starry-eyed poet Galen Madigan hiding
in the mountains, she gave him the care and nurturing he needed.
In return, he introduced her to the magic of love.

CAJUN MAN—Olivia Ferrell
DuBois Electronics was being sabotaged, and Zach had to find
out why. The job intrigued him—and so did Carol DuBois. To
Carol, Zach was spelled D-A-N-G-E-R.

BUTTERFLY AUTUMN—Carolyn Seabaugh
In one single, golden fall afternoon, test pilot Haines Scott taught
Adriana all about butterflies, brass beds, the meaning of her
name—and love. How could she avoid the fluttering of her heart?

GOLDEN GLORY—Stella Bagwell
Lynn hadn't been able to compete with her husband's mistress—
the rodeo. Now, five years after the divorce, she was back—and
still unable to resist the fire of his kiss.

SHEER HONESTY—Susan Phillips
Valerie Dixon could assess a house, but not a man's honesty. So
when John Spencer claimed to be crazy about her, she was
skeptical. Should she trust him, and turn her house into a home?

STRANGE BEDFELLOWS—Arlene James
When Prince Charming turned out to be her political rival, Cal
Brady had trouble trying to view Neal Whitson as her opponent.
She was too busy seeing him as a man.

AVAILABLE THIS MONTH:

Silhouette Desire

Available October 1986

California Copper

The second in an exciting new Desire Trilogy by Joan Hohl.

If you fell in love with Thackery—the laconic charmer of *Texas Gold*—you're sure to feel the same about his twin brother, Zackery.

In *California Copper*, Zackery meets the beautiful Aubrey Mason on the windswept Pacific coast. Tormented by memories, Aubrey has only to trust...to embrace Zack's flame...and he can ignite the fire in her heart.

The trilogy continues when you meet Kit Aimsley, the twins' half sister, in *Nevada Silver*. Look for *Nevada Silver*—coming soon from Silhouette Books.